Eight O'Clock Tales

Entrancing stories for
very young people

Published by Granada Publishing Limited
in Dragon Books 1967
Reprinted 1968, 1969, 1970, 1971, 1974, 1977, 1979

ISBN 0 583 30046 4

First published in Great Britain by
Methuen & Co Ltd 1944
Copyright © Enid Blyton 1944

Granada Publishing Limited
Frogmore, St Albans, Herts AL2 2NF
and
3 Upper James Street, London W1R 4BP
1221 Avenue of the Americas, New York, NY 10020, USA
117 York Street, Sydney, NSW 2000, Australia
100 Skyway Avenue, Toronto, Ontario, Canada M9W 3A6
110 Northpark Centre, 2193 Johannesburg, South Africa
CML Centre, Queen & Wyndham, Auckland 1, New Zealand

Made and printed in Great Britain by
C. Nicholls & Company Ltd
The Philips Park Press, Manchester
Set in Monotype Times

Granada Publishing ®

Enid Blyton

Eight O'Clock Tales

DRAGON
GRANADA PUBLISHING
London Toronto Sydney New York

Roger drove away from Toy-Town

Old Mister Turnabout was always doing good turns to people. He was a nice old fellow, very poor, but always willing to help any one. You would be surprised at the number of good turns he did in a day.

He would help a child across the busy road. He would take a bundle from a tired washer-woman, and carry it for her. He would take any-body's dog for a walk. Really, he seemed to spend his time doing things for other people.

He was a very happy man, for he had dozens of friends. One of his friends was little Billy Smith, the small boy next door. Billy often used to see Mister Turnabout doing his good turns, and he always knew what the old man was going to say when people thanked him for his help. He always said the same thing: "Don't thank me for the good turn I've done you! Just pass it on!"

That was a queer thing to say, wasn't it? "Pass it on!" Billy asked him about it one day.

"Why do you ask people to pass your good turns on?" he asked.

"Because the world would soon be full of good turns if we all passed them on!" said old Mister

Turnabout. "Then we should all be happy and friendly, shouldn't we? And that would be very nice."

"Well, when *I* do a good turn to any one I shall say the same as you do," said Billy. "I shall tell them to pass it on!"

"Yes, do!" said Mister Turnabout. "And you'll notice a very strange thing, Billy. Sooner or later your good turn will come back to you! Yes, it will! It will be a different good turn, but it will be the one that you began!"

Billy thought that was very queer – but old Mister Turnabout knew what he was saying. And this is the tale of Billy's good turn and how it came back to him. Just listen!

The very next day Billy went to play with Wilfred, a great friend of his. They played marbles, and had a grand time. Then they thought they would go and call on Timothy, who lived in the next street, and show him their marbles. So off they went – but dear me, on the way there Wilfred's very best marble, a great big one of blue glass with pink stripes inside it, rolled down a grating into the cellar of a shop.

Wilfred stopped at once and looked through the grating in dismay. Now what was he to do? The shop was empty and locked up, for nobody lived there.

"That marble has gone for ever!" said poor Wilfred, almost ready to cry, because it really was a splendid marble. "The shop is locked up and empty, and there is no way of getting the marble."

But Billy had an idea.

"My Daddy knows the man who has the keys to the shop," he said. "If I ask him perhaps he'll beg for the keys so that I can get your marble for you. I could unlock the shop, go down to the cellar and find it."

"Oh, Billy, but it would be dark down there and lonely," said Wilfred, looking at his friend. "Wouldn't you be frightened?"

"Only a bit," said Billy. "Anyway, I'll try, Wilfred. As soon as my Daddy comes home tonight I'll ask him."

Billy kept his word. He told his father about Wilfred's beautiful marble and how it had dropped down the grating, and he asked him if he might go and get the keys from Mr. White, the caretaker down the road, and find the marble for Wilfred.

"If you like," said his father. He wrote a note to Mr. White and gave it to Billy. The little boy ran off to Mr. White's house, and in a minute or two he had the key of the shop in his hand. Good! Now he could go and hunt for Wilfred's marble!

It was getting dark so he took his torch with him. He unlocked the door of the empty shop and went inside. It was dusty and smelt stale and nasty. Billy found the steps that led down to the cellar and climbed down them. The cellar was full of spider's web and he didn't like it at all. But he really must find Wilfred's marble. He flashed his torch here and there, and at last saw the blue marble in a corner. He picked it up, put it into his pocket and went up the steps again. In a minute or two he was out of the shop and was giving back the key to Mr. White. Then he ran to Wilfred's house with the marble.

"You *are* a brick!" said Wilfred, delighted. "See, Billy, do take one of my little green marbles for getting back my big blue one. You *did* do me a good turn!"

"No, thank you," said Billy. "I don't want a reward for doing a little thing like that, Wilfred. But you might pass on my good turn to somebody else. See? Just give somebody a helping hand when you can. It's a nice feeling – and tell them to pass on the good turn, too, won't you?"

"Yes, I will," said Wilfred. "It's a good idea."

The next day Wilfred was running to buy some sweets from the sweet-shop when a lady in front of him slipped and fell. The bag she was carrying burst open and everything fell out. Papers went flying in the wind, books tumbled out, pencils and pens clattered on to the pavement.

"Oh, dear!" said the lady, and tried to clutch at her papers.

"I'll help you," said Wilfred, remembering that he had a good turn to pass on. So he rushed after the flying papers, picked up all the other things, put them into the bag and handed it to the grateful lady.

She opened her purse to give him a penny, but Wilfred wouldn't take it.

"No, don't give me anything, please," he said. "I'm only passing on a good turn. Will you pass it on to somebody else?"

"What a splendid idea!" said the lady, very pleased. "Yes, I'll certainly pass it on!"

It wasn't long before she was able to keep her word. As she hurried home that evening she saw an old woman standing at the edge of the pavement waiting to cross the road. There was a great deal of traffic rushing up and down the street and the old lady didn't quite like to cross, even when there was a clear space.

The young lady went up to her and took her by the elbow.

"Let me help you over," she said. "You'll be quite safe with me!"

She took the old woman safely across, and smiled at her kindly.

"That was a good turn you did to me, my dear," said the old woman gratefully. "Thank you."

"Then pass it on to somebody else!" said the young lady. "Don't forget! Pass it on!"

The old woman didn't forget. She kept wondering and wondering how she could do a good turn to some one, and at last her chance came.

Mrs. Jones, her next-door neighbour, hung out her washing on the line, and then went off to do her shopping. The old woman happened to look out of her window and was just in time to see the washing-line snap in two! Down went all the clothes in a heap!

"Oh my! Oh my!" said the old woman in dismay. "Look at Mrs. Jones's fine washing! It will all get dirty if something isn't done at once. I'll hurry round and pick it all up myself. I've got a good turn to pass on, and that shall be it!"

She went round the the next-door garden and unpegged all the clothes from the broken line. She was just gathering them all up when Mrs. Jones came back from her shopping and saw what she had done.

"Oh, you kind soul!" she said. "Thank you very much indeed. That's a great help to me. You *have* done me a good turn today! I should have been miserable if I'd come back and found I had all my washing to do again. Thank you for your very good turn!"

"That's quite all right," said the old woman, pleased. "Just pass on the good turn, will you?"

"I certainly will!" said Mrs. Jones.

She didn't forget. She looked out for a chance to do a good turn and it soon came. Old Mr. Lacy across the road was in bed with a bad cold, and Mrs. Jones thought she would make him some good hot soup and take it to him last thing at night, so that he could have it before he went

10

to sleep. So she carried him a basinful that night and he was delighted!

"This is really very kind of you," said Mr. Lacy, gratefully. "I shall enjoy the soup so much, and I am sure I shall have a good night after it. Many, many thanks Mrs. Jones. I hope I shall be able to return your kindness some day, for this is a real good turn you have done me."

"Well, pass it on!" said Mrs. Jones, laughing. "It's a good idea to pass kind turns on, isn't it, Mr. Lacy!"

Now Mr. Lacy lay in bed and thought about what Mrs. Jones had said. He wasn't usually a very kind man. He was really rather mean. But now that he had plenty of time to think about things, he wished he had done more good turns in his life.

"Well, it's not too late to begin," he said to himself. "There's heaps of time to do plenty of good turns even though I am an old man. Now what shall I do? Who is there that I can do a good turn to?"

Mr. Lacy had a toyshop: two people worked for him, a girl in the shop and a man who did odd jobs, delivered parcels, mended broken toys, cleaned the window, did the books, and many other things. Mr. Lacy thought about him.

"Smith will have had twice as much work to do since I've been away with this cold," he thought. "He is a good workman. I think I will

11

do him a good turn. I will ask him if he has any children and I will send a nice toy to each of them. That's how I shall pass on the good turn that Mrs. Jones did me."

He felt quite excited about it. He stayed in bed three days more and then went back to his shop. The man, Smith, had helped the young girl in the shop, and had done all his own work and Mr. Lacy's work too. Mr. Lacy was pleased.

"Have you any children?" he asked Smith.

"Yes, one boy," said Smith, surprised. "He is eight years old and his name is Billy."

"Oh, I was hoping you had three or four children," said Mr. Lacy, quite disappointed. "I wanted to send them each a toy. Well, as you've only one child, Smith, we must choose him a very, very nice toy. What do you think he would like?"

"Oh, Mr. Lacy, how kind of you!" said Smith, surprised and pleased. "Well, there's one thing my boy would be so pleased to have, and that's a good clockwork engine. He's just broken his, and he's so miserable about it. It would be a real good turn to him if you'd let him have another engine."

"I want to do a good turn," said Mr. Lacy, delighted. "See, here is the best clockwork engine in the shop, Smith, and take two carriages and a signal with it. Tell your boy I'm pleased to do him a good turn, and say to him: 'Pass it on!' "

Smith was very anxious to get home that night. Whatever would Billy say when he saw what he had brought him! The little boy had been very sad over his broken engine, but now he would be happy. Smith did up the engine, the two carriages and the signal in a big parcel and ran home all the way that night!

"You're all hot and out of breath, Daddy!" said Billy in surprise. "Why did you run?"

"Because I have a lovely surprise for you!" said his father, smiling. "Undo the parcel and look inside."

When Billy saw the new train and fine signal he was overjoyed. "But did you *buy* it for me, Daddy?" he asked.

"No," said his father. "Mr. Lacy said he wanted to do somebody a good turn, so he asked me to take this home for you. But he said I was to say to you: 'Pass on the good turn!' "

Billy looked at his father in surprise and said: "Oh, how funny! That's what I said to Wilfred the other day when I got his marble for him out of the cellar of that empty shop. Do you suppose it's my good turn come back to me, Daddy?"

"Well, that's a funny thing!" said his father. "I wonder if your good turn *has* been passed on from one to another and has come round to you again. We'll find out! First of all you must ask Wilfred who it was that he did *his* good turn to."

So the next day Billy asked Wilfred.

"Oh, I picked up all the things that fell out

13

when a lady's bag fell open," said Wilfred. "I don't know who she is, but I see her every day. We could ask her if she passed on my good turn, if you like."

So they waited for her that day, and when she came down the road as usual, Wilfred stepped up to her and asked her very politely.

"Oh, I remember!" she said, smiling. "Yes, I did pass on the good turn! I helped an old woman across the busy road just there. It was just about this time of day, so maybe she is doing her shopping again. Look! I do believe that is the old lady over there! Yes, it is! We'll go and ask her if she passed on the good turn."

When they asked the old woman, she nodded her head and smiled. "Oh, yes," she said, "I did pass it on! Of course I did! I picked up all the washing when my next-door neighbour's line broke."

"We'll go and ask her if *she* passed on the good turn!" said Wilfred, feeling very much excited. How wonderful that his good turn should have started so many others!

So they went with the old lady to Mrs. Jones and asked her the great question – had she passed on the good turn?

"Of course!" she said. "I took some hot soup to the old man across the road. If you want to ask *him* about it, you will have to go to the toy-shop in the next street. He will be there."

Off they all went, Billy, Wilfred, and the young

lady, who was just as excited as they were. Mr. Lacy was in the shop, and when he was asked the question he nodded his head and said, yes.

"I sent home an engine and two carriages and a signal to the little boy belonging to Smith, the man who works here," he said. "That's how I passed on my good turn."

"And *I'm* the little boy!" cried Billy. "So my good turn worked all the way round back to me! How marvellous! I must set it going again, because I've still got to pass it on! What fun!"

So the next day he set another good turn going, and said: "Pass it on, please!" Isn't it a fine idea! I'm going to do it too, aren't you?

The Skittle-Policeman

Angela had a box of funny skittle-men. Each man was different. One was a clown with a pointed hat. One was a soldier in red. Another was a sailor in a sailor suit, and a fourth was a policeman in blue. There were nine altogether, and in the box were three balls, red, white, and blue.

Angela used to stand the skittles up in two rows and then she and Nanny used to throw the balls at them and see who could knock down the most. It was great fun.

One day the skittle that looked like a police-man was hit seven times in one morning, and the seventh time a dreadful thing happened. His wooden nose came off! Yes, it did, and it rolled over the floor into a corner. The policeman-skittle was shocked and sad. Fancy having no nose! How dreadful he would look!

When Angela picked him up she squealed in dismay. "Oh, Nanny! He's lost his nose! I don't like him."

"Don't be silly," said Nanny. "I'll find his nose and stick it on for you again. Then he'll be all right."

But they couldn't find his nose, however hard they looked. Angela didn't like the policeman-skittle after that. She said he looked so horrid without a nose, and when Nurse had gone out of the room what do you think Angela did? She threw the skittle out of the window into the garden below! Wasn't it horrid of her?

Poor skittle! He fell into the wet grass and lay there, astonished and hurt. What was he going to do now?

All day long he lay there, and all day long it rained hard! When night came you wouldn't have known the skittle. All the paint had run off him, and he was just plain wood.

When the rain stopped and the moon shone out at night, the policeman-skittle sat up. He looked at himself. Goodness, what a sight he was! He felt his face. No nose! It was really dreadful. He wondered if he could find his nose if he went back to the nursery.

Somehow or other he climbed up the old apple tree by the wall and slipped in at the nursery window. The other toys were playing about on the floor very happily. When they saw the poor skittle-policeman with all his paint washed off him by the rain, they didn't know him.

"Who are you?" they shouted.

"I'm one of the skittle-men," said the policeman, humbly. "My nose was knocked off this morning and I've just come to see if I can find it."

"How awful you look without a nose!" said the golliwog, unkindly. "And you've no paint at all."

"I can't help it," said the skittle, sadly. "It isn't my fault. It's Angela's fault."

"Well, we don't want you back here," said the toys to the poor washed-out skittle. "You look dreadful. Angela threw you away and you must stay away."

"All right," said the skittle, sighing. "Just let me find my nose and I'll go. But I think you're very horrid and unkind."

So they were, weren't they? Nobody helped the skittle to look for his nose, but he found it at last. He picked it up and went to the window.

"Goodbye," he said. "I'm sorry to leave you all."

"Goodbye," said the toys, and they turned

their backs on him and began to play games again. The skittle slid down the apple tree and stood in the grass, wondering what to do.

He began to walk down the garden. He slipped under the hedge at the bottom and found himself in a field. He walked across it and came to a sloping hill-side.

The moon shone brightly. The skittle came to a little ring of toadstools, and then he heard a strange sound of grunting and panting. He looked to see what it was. To his great surprise he saw a small brownie tugging and pulling at the toadstools, trying his hardest to pull them up to carry away. But he couldn't drag the toadstools out of the ground, and at last he sat down on one, sighed heavily and said: "I shall never do it. I shall NEVER do it!"

The skittle felt sorry for the little creature. He walked up to one of the toadstools and tugged. Plip! It came away from the ground at once. In fact it gave way so suddenly that the skittle sat down hard on the ground and said "Oooh!" very loudly.

The brownie saw him and began to laugh. How he laughed! He laughed so much that the skittle began to laugh too.

"I say, I know I oughtn't to laugh at you when you were trying to help me," said the brownie, stopping at last. "But you looked so funny. Who are you?"

"I'm a skittle-policeman," said the skittle.

"I've had my nose broken off, and Angela threw me out of the window because she didn't like me any more. Then the rain came and washed all my paint off me, so I haven't even a uniform on now. I'm afraid I look a dreadful creature."

"You do look rather queer," said the brownie, staring at him. "But you can't help it. I say, aren't you strong? Could you help me to move these toadstools, do you think?"

"Of course," said the skittle. "But why do you want to move them? They look all right just here."

"The silly things have grown in the wrong place," said the brownie. "They should have grown over there, where the magic bus stops — see, by that bush. They are seats for people waiting for the bus."

"Oh," said the skittle, looking in surprise at a bus that suddenly appeared round the bush. It wasn't much bigger than the toy bus in the nursery. It was full of mice, rabbits, and fairies. He stared and stared.

The bus drove off. The brownie began to tug hard at the toadstools again. "Let me do it," said the skittle, and he soon lifted two or three. The brownie carried them to the bus-stop and stood them there in a row. Presently little folk and three mice came along to wait for the bus. They were delighted to find the seats there and soon they were all full.

"It's very good of you to help me," said the

19

brownie, when they had taken up all the toad-stools and moved them to their right places. "I suppose I can't give you a cup of hot cocoa just to warm you up on this cold night?"

"Well, I'm quite warm," said the skittle. "But a cup of hot cocoa does sound very nice."

"Come on, then," said the brownie, and he took the skittle through a tiny door in the hill-side. Inside was a small and cosy room. A fire was burning at the end, and a kettle was singing on the hob. The brownie got out a cocoa tin and made some cocoa. Before long the skittle and the brownie were very friendly.

"It's a pity about your nose," said the brownie. "You would be nice-looking if you had a nose."

"Well, I've got it here," said the skittle. "But what's the good of a nose in your pocket?"

"Oh, you've got it, have you!" said the brownie. "Well, why not let me stick it on for you?"

"Oh, *could* you!" cried the skittle, delighted.

"Of course," said the brownie. "I can get some sticky glue from the buds of the chestnut tree, you know. The bees will go and collect enough for me. They are very clever at getting chestnut glue. Then I can stick your nose on for you."

That night the skittle slept in the brownie's bed with the brownie. He was happy, warm, and comfortable. This was better than living in the nursery with unkind toys and a little girl who

20

threw you out of the window because you had
lost your nose.

In the morning the sun shone. The brownie
went outside and made a strange humming
sound. Soon twelve brown-and-gold bees came
flying up to hear what the brownie had to say.

"Collect me some sticky glue from the chestnut buds," he said. Off they flew. Soon they were
back with the glue and they each put their sticky
gift into a dish set ready for them. The brownie
thanked them and went indoors. He heated the
glue over the fire and then called the skittle to
him. He took the little nose from him, smeared
it with glue, and then stuck it firmly on the
skittle's face. He stuck it on just a little bit
crooked, but it didn't matter – it just made the
skittle look comical and jolly.

"Ooh!" said the skittle, for the glue was hot.
He stood still, quite brave, and in a few minutes
there was his nose, firmly on his face again. How
pleased he was!

"Many, many thanks," he said, looking at
himself in a looking-glass. "That's fine! If only
I could get myself a new coat of paint I should
look just as grand as ever I did!"

"Well, perhaps we can manage that too," said
the brownie, at once. "I know the elf who paints
the bluebells in the spring, and if you don't mind
rather a pale-blue for your uniform, I'm sure she
would come and do it for you."

The skittle-policeman didn't know what to

Ting-a-Ling painted him with bluebell paint

say, he was so pleased and grateful. Tears came into his eyes, and ran down his nose.

"I say, don't do that!" said the brownie, in alarm. "Your nose is only just stuck, you know! If you cry tears, it might come unstuck."

The skittle hurriedly dried his tears and smiled. "You are very good and kind to me," he said. "I would simply *love* a bluebell-coloured uniform."

So the next thing that happened was that they went to call on Ting-a-ling who always painted the bluebells in May. She was pleased to see them and at once agreed to give the skittle a fine new blue uniform. She set to work that same day and you should have seen the policeman-skittle when she had finished. He looked simply beautiful. Really he did.

"You look grand enough to go to Toytown and be the policeman there!" said Ting-a-ling, looking at the skittle, very pleased with her painting. "The policeman there is old, and doesn't know how to deal with all the new traffic that's come in the last few years. You know, buses, trams, trains, motor-cars, and all that. Toytown used to be a peaceful sort of spot, but now it's all different."

The skittle-policeman listened, his eyes shining. How he had longed to be a real policeman and stand in the road with his hand out! But he had never been anything but a skittle, made to be knocked down and set up again.

"Oh," he said. "Oh! If only they'd let me try to do some proper policeman's work in Toytown! How hard I would work! How careful I would be! I would see that no accident happened and that everything went at the right speed."

The brownie and the elf stared at one another in excitement. "Come along!" they suddenly cried to the surprised skittle. "Come along! We'll get you the job! Oh, how pleased Toytown will be to have a new policeman!"

In a trice the skittle found himself being dragged along to the bus at the corner. They all got in and in ten minutes' time they arrived at Toytown. The skittle felt quite at home when he saw golliwogs, teddy bears, dolls, and toy dogs walking about the streets. Every one stared at him in admiration, for he really did look smart in his beautiful pale-blue uniform.

Well, he got the job, of course. The old policeman was only too glad to give it up.

The skittle walked proudly into the middle of the town, where the traffic was thickest, and five roads met. He held up his arm. Everything stopped at once. That was a proud moment for the skittle, I can tell you! He waved his hand. The cars and buses chugged onwards again.

Every one came to look at the new policeman.

"What a beautiful uniform he has!" they cried. "What a lovely nose, just the weeniest bit crooked! Most unusual! How well he guides the traffic! He is a fine policeman, one to be proud of."

What do you think happened one day? A big motor-car came up, driven by a golliwog. At the back were crowded a pack of skittle-men, two dolls, and a teddy bear – and they were all from Angela's nursery, where the skittle-policeman had once lived!

"Honk, honk!" said the car, impatiently, for the golliwog was in a hurry. The skittle-policeman knew that honk, and he looked round sharply. Ah, it was the toys he had once known! They were going too fast. He put up his hand to stop them. The golliwog stopped, frowning. He was afraid of this policeman in his beautiful uniform.

Suddenly the teddy bear gave a squeal.

"It's the policeman-skittle from the nursery. the one whose nose came off! Just look at him! Oooooh!"

The policeman turned round and looked at the toys. He didn't smile. He didn't blink an eye. He just looked at them very sternly.

The toys in the car went pale. They felt uncomfortable. They remembered how unkind they had been. The little doll burst into tears. The policeman-skittle said nothing at all. He waited until the road was clear and then he waved on the motor-car. The golliwog was so nervous that he put on the brake instead of starting the car and the toys nearly fell out with the jerk.

"Come along, now, come along, now," said the skittle in his deepest voice. "Don't hold up the traffic."

The car at last went on. All the skittles stared back at the policeman in fear and admiration. What a grand fellow he was, to be sure! How sorry they were that they had been unkind! Dear, dear, dear, what a mistake they had made! How they wished they were friends with him now!

But it was no use wishing. Once a chance of kindness is lost, it is gone for ever. The toys were very silent that day, and all of them were secretly making up their minds to be nicer in future.

As for the skittle-policeman, how he laughed when he told the brownie and the elf about the toys that night.

"You should have taken them all to prison," said the brownie, indignantly, for he was very fond of his skittle friend now.

"Oh, no," said the policeman. "I just looked at them like this – and they felt dreadful, I know they did!"

"You are a kind and clever fellow," said the elf, and she hugged the skittle. "Let's get married and then I can paint you a new uniform every year when I do the bluebells."

So they are married now, and very happy.

And every day the skittle can be seen in Toy-town, right in the middle of the street, stopping the traffic and waving it on just like any police-man in your own town. Wouldn't you like to see him? I would!

Tick Tock's Tea-Party

Tick-Tock the brownie lived with the enchanter Wind-Whistle, and kept his house neat and tidy for him. He cooked his meals, washed his clothes, and sometimes he helped Wind-Whistle with his spells. He was hard at work all day long, but he was very happy.

One afternoon there came a knock at the door and Tick-Tock went to open it. Outside stood the Princess of the Blue Hills and two of her court, come to visit the enchanter and take his advice.

It was just tea-time and Tick-Tock knew they would all stay to tea – and oh, dear me, what a dreadful thought! – there were no cakes at all, hardly any jam, and just a pinch of tea!

"Pray come inside!" said Tick-Tock, bowing low, for he knew his manners very well. The Princess came in, smelling very sweet and looking very lovely. Tick-Tock gave her and the ladies-in-waiting some chairs in the drawing-room and went to tell Wind-Whistle of his royal visitor.

All the time he was worrying about tea. What should he do for cakes and jam? You couldn't give royal princesses plain bread and butter – and goodness gracious, there was hardly any butter either! It was very worrying.

Wind-Whistle was pleased to hear of his royal visitor. He put on his best cloak at once and said to Tick-Tock: "Get tea ready. Lay it nicely."

"Oh, your highness, isn't it dreadful, there are no cakes, just a pinch of tea, hardly any jam, and not much butter!" said poor Tick-Tock.

"Well, go to the shops and get some," said the enchanter snappily.

"But they're shut this afternoon," said Tick-Tock. "It's early closing day!"

"Dear, dear, so it is," said the enchanter. "Well, never mind. Now listen carefully, Tick-Tock. Lay the table as usual, but place the butter-dish, the jam-dish, and cake-dishes empty on the table – empty, do you hear? Put no tea in the teapot, but fill it with boiling water, I have a mind to do a little magic for the Princess, and at the same time provide a good tea for her."

Tick-Tock listened open-mouthed. How exciting!

He hurried to do what he was told. He laid the table, put out empty butter-, jam-, and cake-dishes, and filled the teapot with boiling water. Then he told the enchanter that everything was ready.

Wind-Whistle led the Princess and her ladies

28

into the room where the tea was laid and bade them be seated. They were surprised to see nothing to eat.

"Madam, do you like Indian or China tea?" began the enchanter, holding up the teapot. Then he caught sight of the brownie Tick-Tock peeping in at the door to watch everything.

"Go to the kitchen!" he ordered. "And shut this door, Tick-Tock."

Poor Tick-Tock! He had so badly wanted to see everything. He shut the door and went to the kitchen – but in half a minute he was back again, peeping through the keyhole and listening to what the enchanter was saying!

"I'll have China tea," said the Princess.

"China tea, pour forth!" commanded the enchanter, and the Princess gave a scream of delight, for pale China tea poured from the teapot into her cup.

"I'd like Indian tea," said each of her ladies, and when Wind-Whistle said: "Indian tea, pour forth!" at once dark Indian tea poured into their cups.

"What sort of jam do you like?" asked Wind-Whistle.

"Strawberry, please," answered his three royal visitors.

"Strawberry jam, appear in the dish!" cried Wind-Whistle. Immediately a great heap of delicious jam appeared.

"And what cakes do you prefer?" asked the enchanter.

"Chocolate cakes for me!" cried the Princess in excitement.

"Cherry buns for me!" said the first lady.

"And ginger fingers for me!" begged the second lady.

"Chocolate cakes, appear!" commanded the enchanter, tapping a dish. "Cherry buns, come forth, ginger fingers, appear!"

Three dishes were suddenly full of the most delicious-looking cakes, and the ladies cried out in delight. Then the enchanter struck the butter-dish.

"Now, butter, where are you?" he cried. Golden butter at once gleamed in the dish. It was marvellous. Outside the door Tick-Tock listened to all this, and tried to see through the key-hole what was happening. It was most exciting.

After tea Wind-Whistle called Tick-Tock to him.

"I'm going to the Blue Hills with the Princess and her ladies," he said. "She needs my help. Look after my house and see that nothing goes wrong. And don't meddle with any magic or you will be sorry!"

By six o'clock Wind Whistle and the ladies were gone and Tick-Tock was left alone. He finished up the cakes that were left from tea and enjoyed them very much. They were much nicer than any that were sold in the shops.

It was whilst he was eating the cakes that the naughty idea came to him. He clapped his hands for joy and danced round the kitchen.

"Why shouldn't I give a tea-party and make all the cakes and things appear!" he shouted. "I can wear the enchanter's magic cloak, and then all the things I say will come true too. Oh, how lovely! Won't I make every one stare! My friends will think *I'm* an enchanter."

He sat down at once and wrote six notes to his friends. One went to Big-Eyes, one to Little-Feet, another to Pippity, the fourth to Gobo, and the last two to Tubby and Roundy the two fat brownies.

"Please come to a Magic Tea-Party," he wrote to each of them. Then he licked up the envelopes and posted the letters. How excited he felt!

He had asked his friends for the next day. So he was very busy in the morning making the house tidy and putting fresh flowers on the tea-table. Then after his dinner he washed himself, did his hair nicely, laid the tea-table with empty plates and dishes, and at last went to put on the enchanter's magic cloak. It was embroidered with suns and moons and shone very brightly.

Tick-Tock walked about in front of the looking-glass in Wind-Whistle's bedroom and thought he looked really very grand.

"Won't I surprise every one this afternoon!" he chuckled to himself. "Dear me! There's the clock striking half-past three! I must put the kettle on for tea."

He ran downstairs, nearly tripping over the cloak he wore, for it was much too big for him. He put the kettle on, and waited for his friends.

They all came together, looking very smart in their best clothes. They were most excited and crowded round Tick-Tock, asking him what a Magic Tea-Party was.

"Wait and see, wait and see!" said Tick-Tock, laughing.

He led them into the dining-room, where tea was laid – but when they saw the empty dishes their faces grew long. Wasn't there going to be anything to eat?

"Wait and see, wait and see!" laughed Tick-Tock, again, running into the kitchen to fetch the kettle, which was now boiling.

His guests sat down round the table, and waited. Tick-Tock came back with the kettle. He was going to do better than the enchanter – he was going to make the cakes, jam, butter, and tea all appear at once!

"What sort of cakes and jam do you like?" he asked his guests. They all called out together.

"Gooseberry jam! Chocolate roll! Coco-nut buns! Cherry cake! Plum jam! Marmalade! Sponge fingers!"

"Right!" said Tick-Tock. He picked up the teapot, which he had filled with nothing but hot water, and then cried out loudly: "Tea, pour forth! Butter, appear! Gooseberry jam, plum jam, marmalade, where are you? Chocolate roll, coco-nut buns, cherry cake, sponge fingers, come forth!"

Then, to the enormous surprise of all his friends, the teapot poured tea into their cups, one after another, jam and marmalade began to come into the dishes, butter heaped itself up in another dish, and cakes fell into a pile on the rest of the dishes. It was perfectly marvellous!

"Wonderful!" cried Gobo.

"How do you do it!" shouted Tubby and Roundy.

"Goodness gracious!" cried the others.

"It's easy!" said Tick-Tock, pouring out his cup of tea last of all. "I'm quite a good magician, you know. I'm sure I could teach Wind-Whistle a lot."

A puzzled look came over the faces of the six guests as they watched the jam, butter, and cakes appearing in the dishes. They had been appearing for quite a while now, and the dishes were much too full. In fact the gooseberry jam was spilling on to the cloth.

"You ought to have put out bigger dishes," said Tubby to Tick-Tock. "Look, they aren't big enough for all the cakes and things."

But Tick-Tock was also feeling puzzled about something and didn't hear what Tubby said. The teapot had filled his cup, but when he set it down on the teapot stand, it didn't stay there. No, it hopped up into the air all by itself and began to pour tea into the milk-jug! It was most peculiar. Tick-Tock took hold of it and put it back on the tray. But as soon as he let go, up hopped the teapot into the air again and poured a stream of tea into the sugar-basin. It was most annoying.

"I say, Tick-Tock, the dishes aren't *big* enough, I tell you!" said Tubby, as he and the others watched the cakes spilling all over the table. "Shall we get some more?"

"No, just help yourselves and eat as much as you want to," said Tick-Tock, still busy with the obstinate teapot. "If you eat up the cakes there will soon be room for them on the dishes."

So the guests began eating – but, dear me, they couldn't eat nearly as fast as those cakes, jams, and butter appeared! Soon the table-cloth was in a dreadful mess, for the jam slid over the edge of the pot and dripped on to the table, and the butter flopped down too, while the marmalade was in big blobs all round its dish. The cakes no longer fell on the dishes as they appeared out of the air, but bounced straight on to the table, scattering crumbs all over the place.

The guests were rather frightened, especially when they saw what trouble the teapot was giving poor Tick-Tock. But they said no more. They ate steadily, though nothing really tasted very

Cakes bounced all over the table

nice. Poor Tick-Tock could eat nothing for all the time he was trying to stop the teapot from pouring tea here, there, and everywhere.

At last it tore itself away from the frightened brownie and poured some tea down Gobo's neck!

"Ow!" squealed Gobo, jumping up in fright as the hot tea dripped down his collar. "Ow! Ooh! It's burnt me!"

He wiped the tea away with his handkerchief and began to cry.

"Hoo, hoohoo! I'm going home! This isn't a nice tea-party."

He ran out of the door and slammed it. The others looked at one another. The teapot moved towards Tubby, but he jumped out of the way.

"Good-bye, Tick-Tock," he said. "I must get home. I've some work to do."

"I must go with him," said Roundy, and the two brownies ran off in a hurry.

It wasn't long before the other guests went too. The magic was frightening them. It was all very well to have as many cakes as you wanted, but to see hundreds dropping on to the table was very queer. They felt sure something had gone wrong.

Tick-Tock was very unhappy and rather frightened. What had happened? Hadn't he done the magic just the same as Wind-Whistle? Why wouldn't everything stop appearing? Why didn't that horrid teapot stop pouring?

Tick-Tock looked round the table in despair. What a mess! Look at all the jam and marmalade! Look at those cakes, not even bothering to fall on the dishes any more! Look at the butter all over the place! And look at that perfect nuisance of a teapot pouring tea on the carpet now! Whatever was he to do?

Poor Tick-Tock! He couldn't do anything. He had started a magic that he couldn't stop. The teapot suddenly stopped pouring tea on the carpet and playfully poured some on Tick-Tock's beautiful cloak. He cried out in dismay.

"Oh! Look what you've done to the enchanter's best cloak! Oh, what a mess! Whatever will he say? Oh, my goodness me, I must go and sponge off the tea at once!"

Tick-Tock rushed upstairs to the bathroom. He took a sponge and began to sponge the tea-stain on the cloak. He was dreadfully afraid the enchanter would see it, and what would he say then? Oh, dear, dear, why ever had Tick-Tock meddled with magic when he had been told not to?

It took a long time to get the tea-stain out of the cloak, but at last it was done. Tick-Tock hung the cloak over a chair to dry and was just going downstairs when he heard some one shouting from outside the house. He stuck his head out of the window to see what the matter was.

Out-of-doors stood Gobo, and he was shouting at the top of his voice.

"Hie, Tick-Tock! Are you all right? There are a lot of funny things happening down here! Look!"

Tick-Tock looked – and out of the front door he saw a stream of tea flowing! Yes, really, it was running down the path! Mixed with it was butter, jam, marmalade, and cakes of all kinds, bobbing up and down in the stream.

"Oooooh!" screamed Tick-Tock, and ran downstairs in a hurry. Well! I couldn't tell you what the dining-room looked like. It was a foot deep in tea, to begin with, for the teapot was still pouring away merrily. And then the cakes! Well, there were hundreds and hundreds of them. The jam and marmalade and butter were all mixed up together, and still more and more things were dropping down into the room.

Tick-Tock waded in. The teapot at once poured some tea on his nose and he gave a cry of pain, for it was hot. Whatever was he to do? This was dreadful.

"Can't you stop the things coming and coming and coming?" shouted Gobo, who was really very sorry for his friend. "You made them start."

"I know," sobbed Tick-Tock. "But I thought they would stop by themselves and they haven't. If only Wind-Whistle was here!"

Then Gobo gave a shout and pointed up the street. "Here he comes!" he cried. "He's come home sooner than you thought!"

So he had. Poor Tick-Tock! He didn't know whether to be glad or sorry. Wind-Whistle strode up the road and when he came to his house and saw the stream of tea pouring out, mixed with jam and cakes, he was most astonished. He stared at it in amazement, whilst poor Tick-Tock tried to stammer all about it.

"What! You dared to meddle with magic when I told you not to!" shouted the enchanter in anger. "You wore my magic cloak! How dare you?"

"Oh, please, your highness, forgive me!" wept the brownie, as white as a sheet. "I just thought I would give a tea-party like you did. It looked so easy. But nothing would stop coming. It just went on and on. The teapot is still pouring in the dining-room."

The enchanter waded through the stream of tea and looked in at the dining-room door. What a dreadful sight! He frowned in anger. Then he clapped his hands sharply three times and said: "Illa rimmytooma lippitty crim!" These words were so magic that Tick-Tock trembled to hear them. But at the sound of them the teapot at once stopped its pouring and put itself in the sink to be washed up. The cakes stopped falling from the air, and so did the jam, marmalade, and butter.

But the dreadful mess remained. Tick-Tock looked at it in despair.

"Aren't you going to make all this mess go too?" he asked his master.

"No, *you*'re going to make that go!" said Wind-Whistle, sternly. "Get brushes, cloths, soap and water, Tick-Tock, and clear it up. It will keep you busy."

Tick-Tock went away howling. The mess would take him days to clear up. But it was his own fault, he shouldn't have meddled with magic. He never would again, never!

Wind-Whistle forgave Tick-Tock, when the house was clean and tidy again. But when he wants to tease the little brownie, he says: "Would you like another tea-party, Tick-Tock, some day?"

But Tick-Tock shakes his head and cries: "No, no, no. Never again!"

The Girl Who Told Tales

Once upon a time there was a little girl who told tales. Her name was Minnie, and nobody really liked her. She was always running to her mother or to her teacher and telling tales about the other boys and girls.

"Mummy!" she would say, "do you know,

Billy Brown put his tongue out at me!"

Or she would go to her teacher and say: "Oh, Teacher, Mary Jones cheated over her sums today. And I heard Mollie talking when she ought to have been quiet."

The teacher was always cross with her when she told tales.

"Leave me to find out these things for myself, Minnie," she would say. "Don't tell tales. It is a nasty habit."

But Minnie didn't stop, so none of the other boys and girls liked her at all. They could have told plenty of tales about Minnie if they had liked – for she was not a very good little girl herself. But they hated tales, and never said anything to their teacher or to their mother when Minnie took a pencil that didn't belong to her, or smacked them when they were playing with her.

One day, when Minnie was coming home from school, she saw a small boy making a bonfire in a field. She watched him, and then, hearing footsteps coming along by the hedge, she looked to see if it were the farmer coming along. It wasn't, but she thought it was.

"Oh, please," she said, "there's a naughty little boy in that field, and he's making a bon-fire."

The little man she spoke to stared at Minnie, and then looked at the small boy enjoying himself.

41

"Have you lost yourself?" asked the little man, who, now that Minnie came to look at him closely, seemed rather queer-looking. He wore a pointed hat with a long feather in it, and a tunic that came down to his knees and was belted with what looked like gold. Minnie stared at him, and he asked her his question again. "Have you lost yourself, I said?"

"What do you mean, lost myself?" asked Minnie, in surprise.

"Well, don't you come from the Land of Taletellers?" asked the little man, sharply.

"No, I don't," said Minnie, beginning to feel frightened. "I live in the village here."

"Oh, no, you must be making a mistake," said the little man, taking hold of her hand. "Come along, I'll take you back home to the land you really come from."

Minnie struggled to get away, but to her enormous surprise everything around her disappeared, and she found herself in what seemed a silvery mist that rushed by her. In a little while it cleared away and Minnie blinked and looked round. She was in a small village, with tiny, crooked houses here and there. Little creatures, with thin, unkind faces were running about on thin legs. They had high, sharp voices and Minnie didn't like the look of them at all.

The little folk ran up to see Minnie. "Who is she?" they cried.

The little folk ran up to see Millie

"I found her in the wrong village," said the man in the feathered hat. "I thought she must be lost, so I brought her here where she belongs. Give her a house and look after her."

"But I don't belong here!" cried Minnie, looking round at the man who spoke – but he had vanished! It was all very queer indeed. Minnie didn't like it. She stared at the sharp-faced little creatures round her and didn't like them either.

"We'll give you a nice house!" they cried. "Come on. You shall live with us in the Land of Taletellers."

Minnie was taken to a small, crooked house not far from where she stood. It had two little rooms in it, one a kitchen and one a bedroom.

"We all have the same," said a Taleteller called Snoop. "Keep your house clean, and come to join us for all meals except supper, which you cook for yourself."

Well, Minnie had to put up with it. It was no use running away because she didn't know where to run to. She didn't like being in that queer little village at all. She found that she was expected to sweep, mop, and dust her house, to light her own fire, and to cook her own supper. She also had to wash her own clothes. All meals but supper were eaten together out of doors, and the little folk took turns at helping to get them.

The head of the village was Higgle, the only

round-faced man in the village. He gave the punishments – the scoldings and the spankings – and he gave the rewards, too, for good work. These were chocolates and fine clothes.

Minnie knew how her own mother kept house, so she hadn't very much difficulty in keeping her tiny house clean. For a few days she swept and dusted very well – and then one morning she got up late, and heard the breakfast bell ringing before she had finished sweeping her rooms properly. So she hurriedly swept the dust under a mat and left it there. Then out she went to have breakfast.

"Do you know what I saw Minnie doing this morning?" suddenly said a Taleteller across the table. "I saw her sweeping all her dust under the mat! Dirty little girl!"

"Ooh, how lazy!" cried every one, and stared at Minnie with round eyes.

Minnie went red and stared angrily all round her. She didn't say anything, but she thought a lot. Nasty little things!

The next day Minnie couldn't find a clean handkerchief, so she tucked a dirty one in her pocket, meaning to wash her others as soon as she could. But a little end hung out and Snoop saw it. He pulled it out of her pocket and showed it to every one.

"Look! This is Minnie's handkerchief. Isn't she a dirty little girl! Fancy not having a clean handkerchief each day!"

"Ooh!" cried every one, in disgust. Then Minnie lost her temper and slapped Snoop hard.

"You nasty taleteller!" she cried. "I hadn't a clean hanky this morning for the first time, and I meant to wash them all today. What do you want to pull it out of my pocket for?"

"She slapped me, she slapped me!" wept Snoop, holding his cheek. "I shall go and tell Higgle."

He ran off to Higgle's house, and Minnie heard him wailing there. She went to her own house, feeling rather frightened. Soon Higgle came stalking up to her door and knocked on it.

"Snoop says you slapped him," he said, sternly.

"Yes, I did," said Minnie, "and he deserved it."

"So do you," said Higgle at once, and before she could say anything more Minnie had a sharp slap too! That *did* surprise her. She burst into tears, slammed her door, and flung herself down on her bed. What a horrid, horrid place this was!

After that Minnie was very careful to have a clean handkerchief each day, and never to sweep her dust under the mat. But will you believe it, those little Taletellers soon found things to say about her again!

"Do you know, Minnie's got a hole at the back of her stocking!" she heard one whisper to another, and then he pointed at her.

"Why didn't you tell *me* instead of him?" cried Minnie. "I didn't know I had one, and I could have gone and mended it."

She mended the hole at once, quite determined not to do anything that would give the Taletellers anything at all to say about her. She knew that Saturday was near, when Higgle dealt out rewards and punishments – and Minnie was very anxious to have a box of chocolates and perhaps a fine pair of shoes with silver buckles like those some of the others were wearing.

She had kept her house beautifully for days. She had done everything she could. She had been polite to the Taletellers, though not friendly, for she really didn't like them at all.

At last Saturday came, and every one lined up in front of Higgle, who was wearing a very grand suit, with buttons of gold all over it.

Most of the Taletellers seemed to have good reports that week, and one after another went up to receive boxes of chocolates or to choose a hat with a feather in it or a pretty coloured scarf. One or two had smackings and went off crying. Minnie longed for her turn to come, for there was a pair of shoes there that she wanted very much indeed. They were just her size, and had bright silver buckles and silver heels. They were really lovely.

"Now, Minnie," said Higgle. "Have you been

47

good this week and done everything you should?"

"Yes, I think so," said Minnie, her eyes on the pretty shoes.

"Please, Higgle, I saw her yawning without putting her hand over her mouth," suddenly cried a little Taleteller.

"And I saw her with a button off her frock!" called Snoop.

"And do you know, Higgle, when it was her turn to do the washing-up on Wednesday she left a bit of mustard on one plate!" cried another.

"And she didn't turn her mattress yesterday when she made her bed!" said another, called Pry, because he was always peeping around.

"How do you know that?" cried Minnie, angrily. "You must have been peeping in at the keyhole as usual, you nasty, prying little thing. Higgle, he's always peeping to see what he can find out. *He* should be punished, not me."

"Well, there isn't really much to choose between you," said Higgle. "He says something nasty about you, and you say something nasty about him. You are both Taletellers, I can see. Come here, Pry, and you shall be spanked for peeping. As for you, Minnie, you can go to your house and put yourself to bed. Nobody seems to have a good word for you."

"Why do you listen to all those nasty tales?"

shouted Minnie, losing her temper. "My mother and my teacher never listened to tales. They said that no nice person ever did pay attention to tales."

"Then why did you tell tales so often!" said Higgle, looking at Minnie with his strange yellow eyes. "I have been told that you were a real Taleteller and would be happy here."

"How can I be happy here with every one saying nasty things about me?" said Minnie, crying.

"But you tell tales about others," said Higgle, puzzled. "Why shouldn't they tell tales about you? A little girl like you who loves to say nasty things about her friends should be very happy here with people just like herself."

"Well, I'm not happy," said Minnie, wiping her eyes. "I want to go back home."

"Oh, no," said Higgle, at once. "You can't go back home when you belong here. Taletellers must live with taletellers, otherwise it isn't fair. When you were at home you told tales about children who were much too nice to tell tales about *you*. So you had things all your own way, and it wasn't right. But here it is all quite fair – you all tell tales about one another. Now stop crying and do as you are told. Go and put yourself to bed for the rest of the day."

Minnie went. She cried bitterly when she was in bed, because she really was very unhappy and longed to go home. "I would never have told a single tale about any one if I'd known there was a land for taletellers," she thought to herself. "How mean it was of Snoop and Pry to tell tales of me this morning – and I suppose it used to be just as mean of me to tell tales of the other boys and girls when I was at home. But they were nice to me and never said anything horrid about me to my teacher. No wonder they didn't like me! I must have been a nasty little girl. Perhaps I still am."

The next day Minnie got up, full of a new idea she thought of. Suppose she went to all the Taletellers and made a bargain with them? Suppose she said to them that if they promise never to tell tales of her she would never tell tales of them? Then things would be much happier.

Every one agreed to her plan and nodded their mean little heads. Minnie was pleased. Now perhaps she would get a box of chocolates and those pretty shoes the next Saturday. As no one was going to tell tales of her she didn't very much bother about her work that week, and her little house was dirty and badly kept. But Minnie didn't care. Higgle wouldn't know because he wouldn't be told!

When Saturday came they all went to him and stood in a line. One after another was praised and given a present, for no one told a single tale. At last it was Minnie's turn. She went up to get her chocolates, but suddenly Snoop cried: "She doesn't deserve chocolates, Higgle! Her house is as dirty as can be!"

"And she hasn't made her bed properly for a week!" cried Pry.

"And she spilt some ink all down the wall!" cried another.

Minnie turned and faced them in rage and disgust.

"You promised not to tell tales of me if I didn't tell them of you!" she cried.

"We know that," said Snoop, "but we thought you'd be good, and you haven't been. So it is our duty to tell Higgle about you."

"It isn't, it isn't!" cried Minnie. "Oh, you horrid creatures! You like telling tales so much that you even break your promises! All right, Higgle, punish me if you like. I *have* been lazy and bad this week, but please let *me* tell you all the bad things I have done, and don't listen to tales about me. I would rather tell you myself, and I will tell you truly."

"Wouldn't you like to tell a few tales about Snoop to pay him out for breaking his promise?" asked Higgle.

"No, I wouldn't," said Minnie. "I am not going to break my promise just because he has broken his. He has been mean and nasty, but that's no reason why I should make myself the same. I shan't break my promise and I shan't tell tales. So there!"

Minnie was sent to her house again and had to stay indoors for two days as a punishment for keeping it so badly the week before. All that week she worked hard. She felt sure that all the Taletellers would find something horrid to say about her, but she didn't care. Let them! They were mean and horrid creatures and they could tell all they liked. She wasn't going to take any notice of them or what they did and she wasn't going to say anything about them, good or bad.

So all that week Minnie did her work well, and was quite polite to the Taletellers. When Saturday came she took her place in the line as usual. She had quite made up her mind that she would never get any chocolates or the buckled shoes.

The Taletellers were angry with Minnie for doing her work so well that they had no tales to tell! So they decided to make up some tales about her. That would be fun!

So when Minnie's turn came you should have heard the tales they told! They were all quite untrue, and Minnie knew they were. She was surprised and hurt to hear what the little creatures said, and she went very red. But she said nothing at all.

"Minnie broke a plate the other day," said Snoop. It was quite untrue – she hadn't.

"Minnie was rude to me on Wednesday," said Pry.

"Minnie took one of my sweets when I wasn't looking," said another.

"Dear me!" said Higgle, looking grave. "What have you to say to these things, Minnie?"

"Nothing," said Minnie. "None of them is true. That's the worst of Taletellers – when they find no tale they can tell, they make one up!"

"Have you any tales to tell about *them*?" asked Higgle.

"None at all," said Minnie, firmly. "I shall never, never tell another tale all my life long! I wish I never had told one. I didn't know till I came here what a horried thing it was to tell tales about others – but now that I see what nasty creatures Taletellers are I've made up my mind I'll stop telling tales, no matter what other people say about *me*!'"

"Dear me!" said Higgle, again, looking at Minnie in a very curious way. "It seems to me, Minnie, that you don't belong here at all."

"I did at first," said Minnie, very red. "I was nearly as bad as the rest of the Taletellers. But I don't belong now. You can keep me here if you like, but you won't ever hear me telling a tale!"

"You can't stay here if you don't belong," said the Taletellers, altogether. "We don't want you! You don't tell tales any more. Go away!"

"I'd like to," said Minnie, and she looked at Higgle. He took up a big box of chocolates, and the pretty pair of buckled shoes and gravely gave them to the little girl. "You deserve them now," he said. "You have learnt a big lesson. You may go back home – but if you should ever feel that you want to tell tales again, we shall be very pleased to see you here and to give you another little house."

Minnie took the chocolates and the shoes in delight. "Thank you," she said. "But you needn't ever expect me to come back again, Higgle. I never shall!"

"You must wait until the man who brought you comes here again," said Higgle. "He will take you home. I expect him today. He is bringing two little boys to live here."

"Oh, poor things!" thought Minnie. "I wish I could just tell them what to do to get away!"

In a short while the man with the feathered hat arrived, bringing with him two small boys. They were pleased to see Minnie and ran up to her. "Do tell us about this land," they begged.

"I haven't time," said Minnie, taking the hand that the man with the feathered hat held out to her. "But just remember this and it will help you – don't tell tales if you want to be happy!"

"But it's sometimes our duty to," said one of the boys.

"It's nobody's duty to tell tales," cried Minnie, and as she spoke she heard her own voice going fainter and fainter. The village of the Taletellers vanished and a silvery mist shone round her. When it cleared the little man was no longer there, and the fields she knew so well were around her. In one nearby was a little boy lighting a bonfire. Minnie stared in surprise.

"Why, did I dream all that?" she wondered. "When I went away that little boy was lighting his fire in the same place. Well, fairy-time is different from ours, so I suppose I've come back to the same place and the same time as when I went away. How queer!"

She stared at the small boy and his fire. But do you know, she never even *thought* of telling a tale about it! It was none of her business. She ran home, and her mother was delighted to see a pleasant face, and to hear no tales at all. What could have happened to change Minnie?

For she *was* changed. Now she is a kindly pleasant little girl, liked and trusted by every one, very glad that she did not have to live for always in the Land of Taletellers. I hope *I* never go there, don't you?

The Runaway Donkey

There was once a gnome who owned a fat grey donkey. The donkey was called Kick-up, because when he was angry he kicked up his hind legs. He had a good home with his master, the gnome,

Twiddle, and although Twiddle was very fond of the donkey, and did all he could to make him comfortable, Kick-up was always complaining.

Once Twiddle bought a dog, but the donkey made such a fuss that he had to sell it again.

"How can I sleep when that dog barks all night?" complained Kick-up. "I won't work for you, Twiddle, if you keep him as well as me."

Then Twiddle tried keeping hens, for he was very fond of boiled eggs. Kick-up kicked up his heels in a fury, and sent a basket of eggs, which Twiddle was carrying carefully, right up into the air – and, of course, all the eggs broke.

"Well, why do you keep those nasty, clucking creatures?" cried Kick-up in a rage. "As soon as I lie down for a snooze in my field those hens lay eggs and start the most terrible cackling I ever heard. Is it such a grand thing to lay an egg? No, it is not. Even snails lay eggs."

"Don't worry yourself," said Twiddle, gently, for he was a good-tempered gnome. "If the hens disturb you, Kick-up, they shall go. I will give them to my next-door neighbour. You know that I am very fond of you, and I want you to be happy."

One day Twiddle dug up a great many potatoes and thought he would take them to market to sell. He had far more than he could eat, and he thought it would be nice to sell some, and with the money buy some paint to make Kick-up's stable smart.

So he spoke to Kick-up and told him that he must take him to market the next day, carrying a load of potatoes.

Now Kick-up had grown fat and lazy. He had planned to snooze in the hot sunshine all the next day, and he was vexed to hear that he was to go all the way to market, carrying a heavy load.

"Master, you work me too hard," he complained. "It is too hot to carry loads to market. I shall get sunstroke and then you will be sorry."

"Then I will get you a sun-hat today," said Twiddle. "I shouldn't like you to get sunstroke, Kick-up, because I am really very fond of you. But you MUST go to market with me tomorrow. I cannot possibly carry the potatoes myself."

"I tell you it is too hot to go to market," said the donkey, sulkily. "If you treat me like this, I shall run away. As for a sun-hat, I don't want one. I should look silly wearing a hat."

But Twiddle was so afraid that his precious donkey *would* get sunstroke, for it was certainly very hot, that he went off to buy a large straw sun-hat for him, with two holes for his ears, and a large pink rose in front, to make the hat pretty. When he got back he slipped it over Kick-up's head, and tied the ribbon firmly under his chin.

"You look very nice," said Twiddle, admiringly. Kick-up jumped up in a temper and ran to the pond. He looked at himself and then flew into a dreadful rage.

"I look foolish, stupid, ridiculous, and a perfect silly!" he shouted in a rage. "Take the hat off at once, Twiddle."

"Who is master, you or I?" said Twiddle, quite firmly, for once.

"I shall run away if you don't take off this hat!" cried the donkey. At that the gnome turned his back on him and walked away, hoping that Kick-up would be in a better temper by the next day.

But do you know, when Twiddle went to Kick-up's stable the next morning, the door was open and Kick-up was not there! He had gone, quite gone.

Twiddle stared in the greatest surprise. Then he looked all round the fields – no little fat donkey was anywhere to be seen. It was terrible. Kick-up had kept his word, and had run away!

Twiddle's eyes filled with tears. He had had the donkey for ten years, and had cared for him and loved him very much. He would miss him dreadfully, even though the little donkey had been so bad-tempered.

"I must see if I can find him," thought the gnome, and he set off for his friends' houses.

"Have you seen a fat, grey donkey wearing a sun-hat?" he asked Gobbo, who was feeding his hens in the back garden. "He's run away."

"Good riddance too!" said Gobbo, at once. "Let's hope he stays away."

"But I'm lonely without him," said Twiddle.

"Poor old Twiddle," said Gobbo. "It's a shame. Look, please will you accept three white hens from me for a present? They will lay you lovely eggs for breakfast, and now that Kick-up is gone there is no one to grumble about their cackling."

"Oh, thank you!" cried Twiddle, pleased. "I shall love to have eggs for breakfast to-morrow."

So he took the hens home in delight and put them into the hen-run. Then off he went to his friend Tiralee, who lived at the other end of the village.

"Have you seen my fat, grey donkey?" he asked. "He's run away, and he's wearing a sun-hat."

"No, I haven't seen him, and I don't want to," said Tiralee. "Horrid thing, he was, with his bad temper and rude ways. You are well rid of him."

"But I'm lonely without him," said Twiddle.

"Poor old Twiddle," said Tiralee, who was very fond of his gentle friend. "Look here, old man, I've got three beautiful puppies here. I'd like to give you one of them to keep you company. He'll grow up into a lovely dog, and be very fond of you."

"Oh, thank you," said Twiddle, gratefully. He took the puppy home and called him Tinker, which the puppy thought was a lovely name.

Kick-up hadn't come back, so off went Twiddle to the next village, to call on his friends there. He knocked at Tiptoes' door, and she opened it.

"Have you seen a fat, grey donkey wearing a sun-hat?" asked Twiddle. "He's run away from me."

"Well, don't have him back," said Tiptoes, at once. "You're well off without him, the bad-tempered creature!"

"But I'm lonely without him," said Twiddle, mournfully. Then Tiptoes was sorry for the little gnome.

"What you want is a cat sitting by your fireside!" she said. "Look, here is a little black kitten for you; it will bring you luck!"

Twiddle was delighted with the cuddly black kitten. He put it under his coat and then went to call on Too-tall, next door.

"Have you seen a fat, grey donkey wearing a sun-hat?" he asked Too-tall. "He's run away."

That's a blessing!" said Too-tall, at once. "I never did like that horrid donkey of yours."

"Yes, but I'm lonely without him," said Twiddle.

"Poor old Twiddle!" cried Too-tall. "I'm sorry for you. Wait a minute. I've two tame pigeons you would simply love. They say 'Coo-roo' all day and are fine company. I'll give you them. They will perch on your hat all the way home, so you won't have any trouble with them!"

Twiddle was delighted with the pretty white pigeons. They perched on his hat at once and were quite at home there, pecking Twiddle's big ear lovingly every now and again.

Last of all Twiddle called on his friend Very-Rich, and knocked at his door. Very-Rich was pleased to see him and shook hands in delight.

"Have you seen a fat, grey donkey wearing a sun-hat?" asked Twiddle. "He's run away."

"Well, you can thank your lucky stars that he's gone, the wretched thing!" said Very-Rich, who had once been kicked by Kick-up, and had never forgotten it.

"But I'm lonely without him," said Twiddle, "and also, it's very, very awkward, because I've a load of potatoes to take to market and I've no donkey to take them now."

"Well, well, well!" said his friend, scratching his head and thinking hard. "Let me see. How would you like me to give you my old pony? I don't need her any more, and she would love to come and live with you. She can carry heavy loads and doesn't mind working at all."

"Dear me, no, I couldn't take a present like that!" said Twiddle

"Dear me, yes, you could!" laughed Very-Rich, and he went to fetch the pony. It ran up to

61

Twiddle and nuzzled its nose into his hand He was so pleased.

"Well, I *would* love to have this pony!" he said. "Thank you very much. I'll treat her very well."

"I know you will," said Very-Rich.

Twiddle climbed up on the pony's back and jogged happily home, with the kitten under his coat, and the two pigeons on his head. What a lot of good friends he had! He certainly wouldn't be lonely now that he had so many animals and birds of his own. Three white hens, a nice puppy-dog, a kitten, two pigeons, and a pony! How lucky he was!

He put the pony into the donkey's stable and told the pigeons they might live there too, and pick up any corn they wished. The puppy he put in a nice little kennel, and the kitten he said might live by the fireside. The hens were very happy in their run.

For a whole week Twiddle and his new friends lived happily together. The pony took him to market and never complained at all. The dog guarded him each night, and always went with him for walks. The kitten sat on his knee and purred lovely things to him. The hens laid him three eggs every day, and the pigeons called "coo-roo" whenever they saw him, and flew down to his shoulders. He was very happy.

Then one night, when Twiddle was fast asleep in bed, the fat, grey donkey came back! He had tried first one master and then another, he had been disobedient and bad-tempered, and he had been beaten and half-starved. He was sorry he had ever left kind Twiddle.

"He'll be glad to see me back," thought the donkey, as he trotted homewards. "He'll have been very lonely without me. He'll treat me better than ever now!"

It was dark when the donkey reached home.

He trotted into the yard and immediately the puppy-dog in the kennel began to bark and flew at him. Snap! He was bitten in the leg and he brayed with pain!

He ran to his stable, but the door was shut. He kicked it open and went inside. But some one else was there – the little pony! He kicked out with his hind feet and the donkey was struck smartly on the nose – biff! Then the pigeons flew down from the rafters and cried "coo-roo" angrily at him, and pecked the tips of his ears!

Poor Kick-up! How frightened he was! This was a dreadful home-coming! He left the stable and went to the house, but on the way he woke up the hens who all started to cackle at once: "kuk-kuk-kuk-kuk-kuk-kuk, a robber, kuk-kuk-kuk-kuk-kuk, a robber!"

Kick-up pushed open the kitchen door, which was never locked. He ran into the kitchen, anxious to get away from all the frightening things in the yard – but the kitten, who was sitting by the fire, flew at him in a rage, dug all her twenty claws into his legs, and spat at him so fiercely that he backed into the kitchen table in fright and over it went!

That woke up Twiddle. Wondering whatever was the matter, he lighted his candle and went downstairs. As soon as the donkey saw him, he cried: "Twiddle, what are all these things you have, that bite, kick, and scratch? Order them away at once! I have come home to keep you company again, because I was sorry to think of you sitting here lonely and sad without me."

"Dear me, but I'm not at all lonely or sad," said Twiddle, sharply. "I have plenty of good company and jolly friends. What have you come back for? I don't want you! You always were a bad-tempered, disobedient, selfish animal, and I don't know how I put up with you. Be off with you! There's no room for you here!"

Kick-up was so surprised that he stood staring at his master, and didn't say a word.

"Go away, I tell you!" said Twiddle, angrily. "What do you mean by disturbing us all at this time of night? If you want to see me in the morning, you may come humbly to me and ask my pardon. I don't want to see you any more tonight."

The donkey ran out of the kitchen and went into the field. It was wet and cold, but he did not dare to go to his stable again. He lay in the field all night, grieving and sighing. In the morning he went to Twiddle again.

"Master," he said, hanging his head, "forgive me. Take me back. Send away these horrid creatures and let me work for you as before I will be a good donkey to you."

"Stuff and nonsense," said Twiddle, patting the puppy and stroking the purring kitten. "I don't want you any more. If you like to live in the field next door and earn your keep by fetching and carrying for me, you can do so. But I don't want you to. I've quite enough animals here already."

Kick-up had to live in the field. He had to work hard. The puppy barked at him. The kitten spat at him. The hens cackled loudly whenever he passed. The pigeons pecked his nose when they could. The pony stood ready to kick; so he wasn't very happy.

But he is learning his lesson. He doesn't complain now. He works hard. He is humble and quiet. Twiddle watches him out of the corner of his eye, because, you know, he really is fond of that silly grey donkey. So I expect he will forgive him one day and take him back – but you may be sure he will still keep his other friends. Ah, it was a good day for him when Kick-up ran away, wasn't it!

There was once a brown teddy bear who was always miserable. You should have seen him! He went about with a long face, his whiskers drooping and his ears down. Nobody knew what was the matter with him, they just knew that he was miserable, and that it didn't seem to be any good to try to cheer him up.

As for the teddy bear himself, he was a foolish fellow. He thought that nobody liked him or wanted him. When he saw the other toys laughing and joking together, giving each other presents, and helping one another, he pulled a longer face than ever. He thought it was too bad that they left him out of everything.

And the toys thought that it was too bad that he wouldn't join in anything – so you see things got worse and worse, and soon the teddy bear went and moped in a corner all day and wouldn't even answer when he was spoken to.

The toys laughed about it at first – and then, because they were kind-hearted, they began to worry about the teddy bear. They sent to the pixie who lived in the pansy bed under the nursery window and asked him for his advice. He was old and very wise.

He peeped in at the window and saw the brown bear moping in a corner, looking very lonely and miserable. He shook his head and thought for a long while.

"I'll tell you the best medicine for him," he said at last. "Give him a great big surprise! That's the best cure for any one who's moping."

"What sort of surprise?" asked the French doll.

"Oh, any kind, so long as it's nice," said the pixie. "That ought to cure him. Don't let him guess what you're doing, though, or that will spoil it."

Well, the toys sat in a corner together and talked about it. What kind of surprise could they give the teddy bear? They really couldn't think of anything!

Then the yellow duck suddenly thought of something. "Why!" she said, flapping her plush wings in delight, "I know! It's the teddy bear's birthday on Saturday. He came from the same shop as I did, and I quite well remember him telling me one day when his birthday was. Couldn't we give him a birthday party? That would be a wonderful surprise!"

All the toys thought the duck's plan was a very good one. So they began to think what they should do.

"I will make the teddy bear a fine blue sash," said the French doll, who was very clever with her fingers. "He will like that to wear at his party."

"And I will make some chocolate buns on the little stove in the doll's house," said the sailor doll, who was really a very good cook.

"I'll make some toffee!" cried the clockwork mouse.

"Sh!" said every one. "The teddy bear will hear you! Remember, it must all be a great surprise!"

The teddy bear heard all the toys whispering together in the corner, and he felt more out of things than ever. What were they whispering about now?

"I expect they are saying horrid things about me!" said the bear sulkily. "Oh, dear, how I wish I didn't live in tbis horrid nursery, with all these horrid toys always whispering horrid things about me. I've a good mind to run away!"

The toys went on with their plans for the party. They decided to build a big house of the pink and blue toy bricks, and to hold the party there. Besides the chocolate buns there should be ginger fingers and sugar biscuits. The pixie promised to bring them some honey lemonade to drink. There were plenty of cups, saucers and plates in the dolls' tea-set for the toys to use. What fun it would be!

They would have games afterwards, and the teddy bear should choose them. The clockwork train promised that if it were wound up it would give the bear six rides round the nursery, which was really a very great treat indeed, for usually the toy train was lazy and wouldn't give a ride to any one at all!

Then there were presents for the bear. There was a fine walking-stick. It was really a pencil with a curved end like a handle, and it belonged to the children whose nursery the toys lived in. But they had thrown the pencil away because it wouldn't write properly. The toys found it and thought it would make a fine walking-stick. So they polished it up and made it shine beautifully.

Then there was a little red and yellow brooch that had come out of a Christmas cracker. It was very pretty and the toys felt sure the bear would like it. There was also a pair of small blue shoes, too large for the smallest doll and too small for the other dolls. They would fit the teddy bear very well, the toys thought.

Nicest of all there was a wonderful little chair, made by the pixie outside, out of bent hazel and willow twigs woven together. That was really a fine surprise.

All the toys were to be in their best clothes. Those that hadn't best clothes, or no clothes at all were to wash themselves well and brush their fur or hair. The party was to begin at four o'clock with a song made up by the golliwog especially for the teddy bear.

The toys were more excited that week than they had ever been before. What whispering there was! What planning! What laughing and joking!

The teddy bear couldn't for the life of him make out what was happening. He tried to listen to the whispering but all he heard was "the party". Then he was more unhappy than ever because he felt sure the toys were going to have a party without him.

"They don't want me," said the poor foolish bear. "They're going to have a party and keep me out of it. The horrid, nasty things!"

Now the toys didn't want the teddy bear to see them building the brick house, or changing into their best clothes on Saturday afternoon in case he guessed their secret. So they decided to ask him to go out for a little walk, and then, whilst he was gone, they could get everything ready for his party.

So the golliwog went to him on Saturday at two o'clock, and said kindly: "Teddy, go for a little walk until four o'clock. It is a sunny afternoon and it will do you good."

The teddy bear went red with rage. So they were going to get him out of the way, were they, whilst they were having their party! They were going to eat everything up! They weren't even going to let him *see* the party!

He rushed out of the door, with angry tears

in his boot-button eyes. It was too bad! He'd run away! Yes, he would!

Off he went down the garden path. He walked and walked and walked. All the time he thought angrily about the toys.

"I *will* run away!" he said to himself. "Yes, I will! But first I'll go back and tell the toys just what I think of them. I'll tell them how horrid they are – how unkind – how selfish! I'll go straight back now and tell them! Then I'll smack that black golliwog on the head and walk out with my nose in the air!"

Back he went to the nursery, quite determined to say some very horrid things. It was just four o'clock when he arrived; the toys had finished getting ready for the party, and were standing in a line ready to sing the song that the golliwog had made up for them.

The bear stamped into the nursery and glared round at the toys.

"I've just come back to tell you what a lot of nast – " he began – but he couldn't finish because at a sign from the golliwog the toys opened their mouths and their beaks and began to sing very loudly:

> "Here's a welcome hearty
> To your birthday party.
> Welcome, birthday-bear,
> Hurry up and share
> In our games and fun
> Till your birthday's done!"

Then they stopped, took a long breath and shouted: "Many happy returns of the day, bear! Many happy returns of the day!"

They crowded round him, shaking him by the paw, and the little pink rabbit gave him a hug! The teddy bear was so surprised that at first he couldn't think what to say.

"But – but – but – is it my birthday?" he asked.

"Yes!" shouted the toys. "And we hadn't forgotten it! We've been having secrets about it all the week. We were so afraid you'd guess. *Did* you guess?"

"Oh, no," said the bear, going quite red to think of all the horrid things he had thought. "I didn't guess for a minute."

"Here's a nice blue birthday sash!" said the French doll. She wound it round his fat little body and tied it in a big bow. He looked beautiful.

"And here's a brooch – and a pair of blue shoes – and a fine walking-stick!" cried every one, giving the surprised bear the presents. The shoes fitted him beautifully, and the brooch looked lovely just under his chin. As for the walking-stick he was as proud of it as he could be. Dear me, could all this be a dream? How lovely! What a silly bear he had been!

They had tea in the splendid brick house. The biscuits, cakes and sweets were most delicious, and the honey lemonade was so nice that the bear had five glasses of it and felt rather like a balloon at the end. But he was so happy that he didn't mind anything.

Then they had games, and after that the bear rode in the clockwork train six times round the nursery. That was lovely. Then he was presented with the chair that the pixie had made for him, and he was so surprised that he could hardly sit down in it! But he did, at last, and it was exactly the right size for him. His very own chair! How proud and pleased he was. He wanted to thank the pixie, so the little creature was called and came in to eat a chocolate bun.

He looked at the bear with a twinkle in his eye.

"Do you know," he said solemnly, "I saw a horrid little bear this afternoon, going along muttering the nastiest things about dolls, and golliwogs, and ducks, and every sort of toy."

The teddy bear looked as red as a tomato. How dreadful! The pixie must have seen him going for that walk!

"But it couldn't have been you, could it?" said the pixie, his bright eyes twinkling more than ever, as he looked at the bear. "It must have been a foolish, sulky, stupid little bear who didn't know what he was talking about."

"Yes, it was," said the teddy bear humbly. "Well, pixie, that little bear will never be so foolish again. I know the toys are my friends,

"Many happy returns of the day, bear!"

and I will be a friend to them. They have given me a lovely birthday, and I will never forget it. It was a wonderful surprise."

"Ah!" said the pixie wisely, smiling round at the listening toys. "A surprise is a fine thing – isn't it, toys? It's a splendid cure for the mopes – and don't you forget it!"

The teddy bear never forgot it. He is always planning lovely surprises for every one, and he never *thinks* of sulking in a corner now!

The Enchanted Doll

Mollie had a pretty doll called Angela, whom she loved very much indeed. She played with Angela all day long, and the only thing she wished was that Angela could talk and walk, instead of just lying or sitting perfectly still, and staring at Mollie with wide-open blue eyes.

"I can pretend you talk to me, and I can pretend you run about and play," said Mollie, "but you don't really and truly – and it *would* be such fun, Angela dear, if just for once in a way you would really come alive!"

But Angela just sat and stared, and didn't move a finger or say a word! It was most disappointing, for she really was a nice doll, and Mollie felt quite certain that if only she *could* talk and walk, she would be a jolly companion to have. Mollie had no brothers or sisters, so she was often lonely. That was why she played so much with Angela.

One day a very strange thing happened to Mollie. She took her doll for a walk in Pixie Wood, and it happened there. Mollie had never seen any pixies or anything at all exciting in Pixie Wood, although it had such a lovely name. It was just like an ordinary wood.

But today it seemed a little different. The trees seemed closer together, as if they were nodding to one another, and whispering about something. The sun couldn't get in between the branches, and the wood was dim and rather mysterious. Mollie took Angela by the hand and walked her over the grass, talking to her. Her doll's pram was broken and had gone to be mended, which was why Angela was not riding in it as usual.

Mollie walked on through the wood – and then she suddenly stopped short. She saw something most surprising in the wood! It was a tiny pram, a little smaller than a doll's pram, and it shone like pure gold. It had a little white hood with a silver fringe hanging down, and the pram cover was white too, with gold embroidery on it. It really was very beautiful.

"Whatever is a doll's pram doing here in the middle of the wood?" wondered Mollie. "I haven't seen any other children about. I wonder if they've left their pram here and are playing hide-and-seek or something. I'll cuckoo to them and see where they are. Perhaps they would let me play with them."

So she called loudly: "Cuckoo! Cuckoo! Where are you? Can I play with you?"

But there was no answer. The trees seemed to lean closer to one another, and all the leaves whispered again. Mollie looked all round and ran here and there, but it was no use at all – she couldn't see any children.

She looked at the lovely little pram. It was the nicest she had ever seen. How pretty Angela would look if she were tucked up in it and taken for a ride! Mollie went over to the pram and turned back the cover. There was no doll inside – but would you believe it, there was a little bottle there full of milk!

"But this pram can't belong to a *real* baby! It can't!" cried Mollie, in astonishment. "It's too small. Oh! I wonder – I just wonder if it belongs to a pixie! It would be just right for a pixie baby. Oh, how lovely! I wish, I wish, I wish I could see a real pixie baby riding in that dear little pram!"

Mollie waited for a little while to see if any one came, but nobody did. Then a thought slid into her mind – would it matter if she put Angela into the pram and just wheeled her about for five minutes? Angela must be tired with her long walk, and really, she would look perfectly sweet in that pram! It wouldn't spoil the pram.

So Mollie picked up Angela and put her into the pram. She sat her down firmly, strapped her in, and set the soft pillow up behind her so that she could sit up comfortably. Then she tucked the white cover round her and began to wheel her about. How pretty Angela looked in the pixie pram! It was most exciting to wheel her about in it.

Mollie gave Angela a ride for a few minutes and then she thought she saw a little pointed face peeping at her from behind a tree.

"Who's there?" she called. "Come and see Angela in this dear little pram, pixie!"

There was no answer – so Mollie left the pram and ran to the tree to see if the pixie really was peeping there. But, wasn't it disappointing, there was no one there at all, except a scurrying rabbit with a white bobtail!

Mollie turned back to the pram, and oh dear me, what a shock she got! The pram was running away! Yes, it really was! It was wheeling off all by itself, between the trees, as fast as ever it could!

"Oh! Oh! Come back, come back!" shouted Mollie. "Angela, Angela! Oh, please, pram, do come back! Don't take Angela away!"

But the pram hurried on. Mollie wondered if an invisible fairy was wheeling it, or whether the pram was a magic one that could go by itself. Oh, why, why had she put Angela in it! She ran after the hurrying pram as fast as ever she could, shouting as she went. The pram went faster and faster. It was dreadful. Mollie caught sight of the doll's face. It was full of horror and fear, and the little girl was sorry for her doll. She must, she really *must*, catch that pram!

The pram turned a corner by some thick bushes, and disappeared from sight. Mollie panted after it, but alas, when she reached the bushes, she could no longer see the pram. It was quite gone!

Mollie ran wildly about, and began to cry when she could not see the pram anywhere.

"Where have you gone, Angela?" she shouted. "Can't you call and tell me?"

But there was no answer. Angela had disappeared with the pram. Mollie sat down and cried bitterly. It was dreadful to lose her doll like that. She did love her so much.

Presently she left a little hand on her shoulder and a high, twittering voice said: "What's the matter? Would you mind getting up? You are sitting on my front door."

Mollie looked up in surprise. She saw a tiny creature by her, with long, pointed wings, pointed ears, and pointed shoes. It was smaller even than Angela, her doll, and was looking at her with big green eyes.

"Are you a pixie?" asked Mollie, in astonishment. "How sweet you are! Am I really on your front door? I'm so sorry."

She got up, and saw that she was sitting on a small yellow trap-door, sunk deeply into the ground. The pixie opened it and then looked at Mollie.

"Why are you crying?" he said.

Mollie told him all about the little pram she had found, and how it had run off with her doll.

"Oh, that pram belongs to Mother Dimity, the old woman who lives in a shoe," said the pixie at once. "She is very forgetful, you know, and leaves it about everywhere! If she goes home without it, she whistles for it and it goes to her of its own accord."

"Well, it's taken my doll too," said Mollie, beginning to cry again. Her tears fell in at the pixie's trap-door and he frowned.

"Please don't do that," he said. "You are making my home all damp. Why are you crying now? You can easily go and find your doll. Mother Dimity will give her back if you ask her."

"Where does she live?" asked Mollie.

"In the Shoe," said the pixie, getting into his trap-door home. "Knock at the Big Oak-Tree six times, go down the steps, find a boat to take you on the Underground River, and then ask the Wizard Who Grows Toadstools where the Shoe is. He is sure to know, because the Old Woman is his sister."

"Thank you," said Mollie, getting up. The pixie said goodbye and shut his trap-door with a bang. Mollie looked round for the Big Oak-Tree. There were a great many oak-trees around, and they all seemed about the same size to the little girl. She chose one that looked a little bigger than the others and knocked six times. Nothing happened at all. She knocked again. Still nothing happened.

"It can't be the right tree," said Mollie, disappointed. She looked round again – and then she saw the biggest oak she had ever seen in her life! It was a real monster, towering up into the sky, and as big round as a summer-house!

"That's the one!" thought Mollie, and she ran over to it. She knocked on the trunk sharply six times – rat-tat-tat-tat-tat-tat! Then there came a creaking noise, and to her great delight a small door swung open in the tree and she saw that a narrow flight of steps led downwards towards the roots.

Her heart beat fast. This was a wonderful adventure! She slipped through the door, which at once shut with a bang, and began to go down the steps. It was rather dark, but small lanterns hung here and there gave a little light. Mollie went down for a long way. She thought she must have climbed down quite a hundred steps when she came to a wide passage, with doors on every side. She looked at them. They all had

81

names on, or messages written on little cards.

One card said: "Ring, don't knock." Another said: "Knock, don't ring." The next door had a card that said: "Don't knock or ring," and the fourth one said: "I am not at home yesterday or tomorrow."

Mollie thought that was strange, and she giggled. The names were strange too. "Mister Woozle" was on one card, and "Dame High-come-quick" was on another. Mollie read a third one, "Little Jiggy-jig," and she was just wondering whatever he could be like when his door flew open and some one rushed out and nearly knocked her down. It was Little Jiggy-jig himself!

He was a funny fellow, with small wings, rabbit's ears and a funny habit of jigging up and down. "Sorry!" he said to Mollie. "Didn't see you there!"

He was just about to rush away when Mollie caught hold of his arm. "Wait a minute," she said. "Could you please tell me if I am on the right way to the Underground River."

"Yes, yes," said Little Jiggy-jig, jerking his arm away impatiently. "First to the right and left and then straight on round the corner."

"But how can I go to the right and left at once, and how can any one go straight round a corner!" called Mollie, indignantly. The only answer she got was a chuckle, and Little Jiggy-jig disappeared into the darkness of the passage.

Mollie felt cross. She went straight on, and at last heard a noise of lapping water. "That must be the Underground River," she thought, pleased. "Now to find a boat!"

She soon came to the river. It was hung with fairy lights of all colours and looked very pretty. There were plenty of boats on the side of it, but none of them had oars in them. Mollie looked about for some one to row her down the river, but she could see no one.

"Isn't there any one here?" she shouted. Then a little head came poking out of a funny little ticket-office Mollie had not noticed.

"Yes, I'm here, and you're here too," said the person in the ticket-office. Mollie went up and saw that it was a grey rabbit with a collar round its neck, and a tie flowing down, very neatly knotted.

"Good morning," said Mollie. "I want a boat."

"Here's your ticket, then," said the rabbit, handing her a very chewed-looking piece of cardboard.

"Where's the boatman?" asked Mollie.

"Nowhere," said the rabbit. "There isn't one."

"Then how can I go in a boat?" asked Mollie.

"Get in it yourself, silly," said the rabbit.

"Don't be rude," said Mollie. "It's no use taking a boat if you haven't got oars, is it? Silly yourself!"

"Now who's being rude!" said the rabbit.

"You are being very simple, little girl. Why do you want to take a boat? Why not let the boat take *you*?"

Mollie glared at the rabbit, and then walked up to one of the boats. She chose a blue one, dotted with gold stars and got into it. At once the boat glided off by itself.

"Good morning, good afternoon and good evening!" shouted the rabbit, but Mollie didn't answer. She thought he was rather silly.

The boat shot on down the river, and after a little while it left the underground darkness and came out into the open air. Mollie blinked in the bright sunshine, but she was very glad indeed to be in the light again. The boat sped on and on, and Mollie watched the queer folk walking in the flowery fields, and saw with surprise that the animals were dressed up like human beings.

The boat went on, rocking gently. Mollie suddenly saw a curious field, with a strange-looking old man waving a stick about in the middle of it. She saw that he was surrounded by toadstools of all sizes, colours, and shapes, and she knew that he must be the Wizard Who Grows Toadstools.

"Stop, stop!" she cried to the boat. It stopped at once and headed to the bank. Mollie patted it, said thank you and then jumped out. She went to the old wizard, who didn't see her at first and almost knocked her over with his waving stick, which the little girl now saw was a silver wand.

"Please," she said. "I've come to ask you where your sister, the Old Woman Who Lives in a Shoe, is. I want to go and speak to her."

"You'll find her on the other side of that hill," said the wizard, waving his wand violently, and nearly catching Mollie in the eye with it. "Look out! You are standing just where my next toadstool is growing!"

Mollie felt the earth pushing up under her feet and fell over. A big toadstool appeared through the ground and grew high and broad. It was covered with big red spots. Mollie sat on the ground and watched it in amazement. Then she felt the earth moving just under her again, and in a trice she was shot up high on another growing toadstool.

"Well, really," said the wizard, in disgust, "how you do get in the way, to be sure! Mind where you tread as you go through the field. There are toadstools growing everywhere today, for I have a very large order for them from the King himself, who wants three hundred for stools for his next party."

Mollie ran out of the field as quickly as she could, and made her way to the hill in the distance. She climbed it, and as soon as she came to the top she saw the Shoe. It was an enormous shoe, and it had windows and doors in it and a smoking chimney at the top. Mollie

"Well, really," said the Wizard, *"how you do get in the way!"*

thought it looked lovely. She ran down to it, and at once she was surrounded by a crowd of small pixie children, not so big as she was, with pointed faces, pointed ears, and short wings.

"Who are you? Where do you come from?" they cried in excitement. "Have you come to see our new child?"

"Look, our new little girl is in bed! You can see her through the window!" said a tiny pixie, taking Mollie's hand and leading her to a window that looked into the Shoe house. Mollie peeped in – and whatever *do* you think she saw? She saw a bedroom in the Shoe, with many little white beds in it, and in one of them, the bed nearest to the window, lay Angela, her own little doll!

"Do you see that new little girl?" said the pixie. "Well, she came today in Mother Dimity's pram, and do you know, she is very ill, poor thing! She can't talk, she can't eat, she can't drink, she can't even blink her eyes! Isn't it dreadful! I've never seen a little girl like that before, have you?"

"That isn't a little girl at all, that's my doll!" cried Mollie.

"A doll!" said the pixie children, crowding round Mollie. "What's a doll? We don't know what a doll is."

"Well, a doll is – a doll is – well, that's what a doll is!" said Mollie, pointing to where Angela lay on the little bed.

"But can't the poor things move or talk at all?" asked the pixies in surprise.

"Of course not," said Mollie. "I'm going in to get Angela. Poor darling, she must feel so frightened!"

She ran in at the door of the big Shoe, and bumped into the Old Woman.

"Now then, gently, gently!" said Mother Dimity. "You'll frighten the new little girl, rushing about like that. I've just given her some very strong magic medicine to make her come alive again."

"She never has been alive!" cried Mollie. "She's my doll!"

"Your doll!" said the Old Woman. "Doll! Oh, I remember once seeing a doll in the world of boys and girls. Dear, dear me, so that's a doll, is it? Why, I thought it was a little girl that was ill, and so I've given her some stuff to make her walk and talk. I'm really very sorry indeed."

"But, do you mean to say that Angela will soon walk and talk?" cried Mollie.

"Of course," said Mother Dimity. "Look – she is blinking her eyes now! Perhaps I had better make her go back into a doll again."

"No, please don't," said Mollie at once. She ran to Angela and looked at her. Wonder of wonders, the little doll was opening and shutting her eyes and she suddenly looked at Mollie and smiled a wide smile, showing all her pretty teeth.

"Hallo, Mollie, dear," she said. "I've often wanted to talk to you, and now I can!"

Mollie watched her in amazement. Angela threw back the covers and jumped out of bed. She danced round the room in joy and then ran up to Mollie. She hugged the little girl's legs, and Mollie lifted her up into her arms. She was so pleased to have Angela back, walking and talking, that the tears ran down her cheeks in joy.

"Oh, what fun we'll have together now!" she cried, hugging her doll to her. "We can talk to one another, and play all kinds of games."

"But you mustn't let any one but yourself know," said Mother Dimity at once. "If you do, the magic will go, and Angela will be an ordinary doll again."

"Oh, I won't tell any one at all!" said Mollie, happily. "Come, Angela, we'll go home again now. It must be getting late."

She put the little doll on the ground and Angela took her hand. Then, walking like a real person, she trotted beside Mollie, saying goodbye to all the pixie children.

Mother Dimity showed them a short way home, and they arrived there just in time for dinner. Mollie put Angela in her cot, and told her to be sure not to move if any one came in, and she promised.

And now Mollie is as happy as the day is long, for she has a real, live doll to play with her, and they *do* have some fine games together.

"Really!" Mollie's mother often says, "you might think that doll was alive, the way Mollie plays with her all day long!"

And then Mollie smiles a big smile – but she doesn't say a word! She has a wonderful secret to keep and she keeps it very well!

The Very Clever Rabbit

Willy had a big black rabbit with a woffly nose, and a white bobtail. He called her Loppy, and was very proud of her indeed. She was a very clever rabbit, and Willy taught her a lot of tricks.

When he brought her a nice fresh lettuce she would sit up and beg for it, and until he said: "It's yours, Loppy," she wouldn't touch it. Then she would drop down on all-fours and nibble at it.

When Willy said: "Turn round and show your white bobtail!" Loppy would turn right round and stay there till Willy said: "Now you can look at me again!" Wasn't she clever?

She could do other things too. Willy used to let her out of her nice big cage for a run on the lawn with him, and when he said: "Follow at heel, Loppy!" she would follow him all round the garden close to his heels just like a good dog. His mother used to laugh when she saw them going for walks together down the garden paths.

Loppy always came when she was called. If she was nibbling the grass at the other end of the garden, and Willy called: "Loppy! Come here!" she ran to him at once. She loved Willy very much, and he loved her. She couldn't talk, but when she put her soft chin into Willy's hand and he felt her nose woffling against his fingers, he always knew exactly what she was thinking.

When Willy was nearly seven his father said that Miss Brown, who had been teaching him to read, must go, and Willy must join the boys' school in the town.

"But what will Loppy do without me?" asked Willy at once. "She will be terribly lonely. I shall be away all day."

"Oh, she'll soon get used to that," said Daddy, smiling. "You can't possibly take her to school with you, you know."

"But she *will* be lonely," said Willy. "Daddy, could I get another rabbit to keep her company? Then she wouldn't be so lonely."

"No," said Daddy. "Loppy will be all right, don't worry. She won't miss you after a bit. You can always go and talk to her when you come home from school. One rabbit is quite enough for you to look after, especially now that you are going to school."

91

Willy knew it wasn't any good saying any more. Daddy wasn't very fond of rabbits, and he didn't understand how Loppy would feel. He told Loppy all about it, and she put her nose into his hand, and listened very sadly.

Soon the time came for Willy to go to school. He was to stay to dinner each day, so he only saw Loppy for a few minutes in the morning before he went, and then for a little while when he came back, for he had homework to do in the evening, and that didn't leave him much time for play.

He went to school on Saturdays too, so there was only Sunday left for Loppy, and by the time Willy had been to church and Sunday school there didn't seem any time left at all. He was a terribly busy little boy.

He missed Loppy very much and she missed him too. She grew thin and mopy and was always watching for a little boy who could seldom come. Willy was sad, and he did wish that Daddy would let Loppy have another rabbit for company.

He asked Mummy about it, but she said that if Daddy had said no, she couldn't possibly say yes. But she would ask him and see if she could get Daddy to change his mind.

"Certainly not!" said Daddy. "Willy has got to work hard now, and I don't want his time taken up with too many pets. Loppy's all right. Whoever heard of a rabbit pining?"

"Well, Loppy certainly seems thinner than she was," said Mummy. "I don't think it would take Willy much more time to look after two than one, Daddy."

"I've said no, and I mean no," said Daddy, and then Willy knew it wasn't a bit of good worrying about Loppy any more.

One day the boys at school began to talk about their pets.

"I've got a dog," said Jack. "He's a fine dog, I can tell you! Do you know what he does? He sits up on his hind legs, waves his front ones in the air and balances a biscuit on his nose!"

"Well, you should see my cat!" said another. "She's called Whiskers because of her beautiful whiskers. If I say 'Mouse!' to her, she runs to the mouse hole in the kitchen and puts her paw into it!"

"Well, my pony is cleverer still," said Peter. "When I say 'Dance!' he stands up on his back legs and sort of waltzes all round in time to my whistling. What do you think of that?"

"*I've* got a clever rabbit," said Willy, proudly.

"Oooh! A rabbit is stupid. It's never clever. It's got a nice up-and-downy nose, but that's all that's clever about it!" said Jack.

"Well, I tell you Loppy *is* clever!" said Willy. "She can beg like a dog, she turns round and shows her white bobtail when I tell her to, and she always, always comes when she is called, even if she is right at the other end of the

93

garden. And she will follow at heel, too, just like a dog, when I tell her to!"

"Story-teller! Oh, the story-teller!" cried all the boys, laughing.

"I'm *not*!" said Willy, going red. "My rabbit can do all those things and others too. I taught her."

"There isn't such a clever rabbit in the world," said Jack. "So we don't believe you. You're a fibber. Say you're a fibber!"

"I won't!" said Willy, fiercely. "I'm not a fibber. I'm telling the truth. You can all come and see my rabbit, if you like, then you'll know I'm telling the truth."

"Well, ask your mother if we can, and we jolly well will!" said Peter.

Mother said the boys might come and see Loppy the next afternoon. Willy went to tell Loppy, and found her looking very sad and lonely. He put her through all her tricks and talked to her kindly. But she wouldn't cheer up.

And wasn't it a dreadful thing – when he brought all the boys to see her the next afternoon, she wasn't there! Her cage door was open, and Loppy was gone.

Willy had such a fright. He called and called, but she didn't come. She was quite gone.

"There!" said Jack scornfully. "You said she always came when she was called, and she doesn't. You are a story-teller. I don't believe you've got a rabbit."

Willy hardly heard what Jack said. He was so upset to find Loppy gone that he really didn't know what to do. He told the boys to go home, and then he began to hunt for Loppy. But she wasn't in the garden. She wasn't anywhere that he looked, not even in the lane outside the garden gate.

"She's run away because she is lonely," said Willy, miserably, and if he hadn't been a big boy, going to a proper boys' school, he might have cried. But, of course, he didn't.

"She must have gone away to the common," said Willy to himself. "There are lots of rabbits there, because I've seen them. She would find heaps of friends there. Oh, I do hope she comes back!"

But she didn't. The boys teased Willy dreadfully and said she was only a make-believe rabbit, and called him a story-teller again. Willy didn't know what to do. Then one day he had an idea.

"I'll go to the common every morning early, before breakfast," he thought. "I'll go to a different place each day, and I'll call Loppy. If she is anywhere near where I am calling, I'm sure she'll come to me!"

So each morning, very early, he started off to the common, and called: "Loppy! Loppy! Loppy!" But no rabbit came running to him. He saw lots of sandy-grey ones, but never a black one at all. It was very disappointing.

One Monday morning he went to a little hilly place on the common and looked round. This seemed a good place, he thought. He began to call loudly:

"Loppy! Loppy! Loppy!"

And whatever do you think? A little black, woffly nose peeped out of a rabbit-hole, and then a big black rabbit ran joyfully out and cuddled up against Willy's feet. It was Loppy!

Willy was so glad that he laughed out loud for joy. He lifted Loppy up and stroked her. She put her chin into his hand and woffled her nose against his fingers just as she always used to do.

"Oh, Loppy, do come back home with me. I've missed you so," said Willy. "If I say 'Follow at heel!' as I used to do, will you follow, I wonder? I'll try."

He put the big black rabbit down gently, and then spoke to her. "Follow at heel, Loppy!" Loppy ran a few steps after him and then stopped. She turned her head towards the rabbit-hole she had come from and then looked up at Willy.

"Do come, Loppy," begged Willy. "Follow at heel!"

But Loppy didn't. She suddenly turned and ran back to her hole, and Willy could have cried with disappointment. He stood there, not knowing what to do.

And then – Loppy came out again. And

behind her came – what do you think? Eight small baby rabbits! Two were black, like herself, two were brown, and four were black and brown mixed. They were all very pretty and Loppy looked very proud of them!

Willy couldn't believe his eyes. Eight little rabbits, and all belonging to Loppy. What a marvellous thing! Loppy ran up to him, and all the little rabbits sat round in a ring and watched to see what their mother wanted them to do.

Willy walked a few steps. Loppy came after him and all the babies followed. Willy walked a little farther. They followed him. Then he walked all the way home, and will you believe it, Loppy kept to his heels all the time and the baby rabbits followed in a long line, hoppety-hopping behind their black mother. It was the funniest sight.

It was a good thing it was so early, and there were no dogs about. A milkman saw the rabbits and stared as if he couldn't believe his eyes – and then Willy met two boys of his school. They had been for an early bathe in the river, and when they saw Willy with Loppy at his heels, and a whole string of young rabbits, they stopped and stared at them with their mouths wide open.

"Don't come near!" said Willy. "You might frighten them. I want to get home safely. I told you I had a clever rabbit, didn't I?"

Daddy was shaving at the bathroom window when Willy came in at the garden gate. He gazed and gazed at the strange sight of Willy being followed by nine rabbits. He saw Willy go up to the cage, open the door, and lift Loppy inside. Then one by one he gently lifted up each baby rabbit too, and shut the door.

"Willy! Whatever has happened?" shouted Daddy.

"I'll come and tell you, Daddy," said Willy, happily, stuffing a fresh lettuce into the cage-wire. Then he ran indoors and told Mummy and Daddy all about it.

"You'll let Loppy have her little rabbits with her, won't you, Daddy?" he asked.

"Well, I never in my life heard or saw such a queer thing!" said Daddy. "Yes, Loppy can keep her babies, of course. I'll write to the papers about the amazing way they all followed you home."

He did, and some one came to take Loppy's photograph and she made a lovely picture with all her black and brown children round her. It was all in the paper, and Willy's school-friends read it, and knew that he had spoken the truth. Besides, the two boys he had met on Monday morning soon told every one about it, and Willy was asked such a lot of questions.

"We're sorry we called you a fibber," said Jack.

"That's all right," said Willy, delighted to have the boys so nice to him. "Mother says I can have two of you to tea each day, so that you can all see Loppy and the little rabbits."

"Hurrah for Loppy!" cried the boys. "She really is a wonderful rabbit!"

And she is, isn't she? She isn't a bit lonely now, you may be sure, with eight beautiful children to keep her company.

All The Way To Toy-Town

One morning Roger thought he would go for a ride in his little motor-car. It was a fine car, painted a bright green, and it had a hooter, two lamps, and a little extra seat at the back for one passenger. Roger was very proud of it. He had had the motor for his birthday, and he could work the pedals so quickly that the car shot along the road at a tremendous pace!

"I'm just going for a ride, Mummy!" he called to his mother, climbing into his car. "I shan't be long."

Off he went, pedalling fast down the lane. He thought he would go through the wood. The path was narrow, but just big enough for his little motor-car. There might perhaps be a few blackberries just beginning to get ripe.

Into the dim green wood he went. A rabbit ran across the path and Roger hooted at it, "honk, honk!" He didn't want to run over a bunny! On and on he went and at last stopped in surprise.

He must have taken the wrong turning! He didn't seem to know this part of the wood at all! He began to turn his car round so that he could go back – and it was just then that he heard the sound of some one crying nearby.

"What's that, I wonder?" said Roger to himself. "Perhaps it is somebody lost."

He jumped out of his car and went to see. Behind a tree he saw a small and very pretty little girl, her golden hair all over her face, as she bent her head and cried into a little pink handkerchief.

"I say!" called Roger, "what's the matter? Are you lost?"

"No," said the little girl, looking up in surprise. "I know my way all right, but I can't walk any farther. So I'm crying because I am unhappy."

"Why can't you walk?" asked Roger. "Have you hurt your foot?"

"Well, you see, my leg has come right off," said the little girl, much to Roger's astonishment. "Don't look so surprised, boy. I'm not a little girl – I'm a doll, and dolls' legs easily come off, you know, if people are careless with them."

"A doll!" said Roger, still more astonished. "I didn't know dolls could talk and walk."

"Well, they can't usually," said the doll. "Only when something important has happened. You see, Mary, the little girl I belong to, dropped me yesterday and my leg almost broke in half. So last night I made up my mind to go to Toy-Town and get it mended. They have a fine dolls' Hospital there. But on my way my leg got worse and now, look, it's come right off!"

Roger looked – yes, it was true. The doll's leg *had* come off. No wonder she couldn't walk any more!

"Won't it push back into place?" he said, knowing that sometimes the arms and legs of dolls could be mended like that. But the doll shook her head.

"I'm afraid not," she said. "I'm not that sort of doll. But really, I don't know what in the world to do! I can't walk back home to Mary, and I can't get to Toy-Town. And if I stay here I shall be ill with cold and loneliness!"

"Where is Toy-Town?" asked Roger. "If you know the way perhaps I could take you there in my motor-car."

"Ooh! What a lovely plan!" cried the doll, delighted. "I didn't know you had a motor-car. I thought you were just walking. Of course you can take me, if you don't mind!"

Roger helped the doll to her one foot. She carried her broken leg under her arm and didn't really seem to mind much about it. She hopped to the car and got into the little seat at the back. Roger climbed into his seat and pedalled off through the wood.

The doll knew her way very well indeed. "Now round this beech-tree," she said. "Now keep straight on till you come to a little gorse-bush. Now to the left by that hazel. Now round the corner by that tiny stream. You'll have to go through it, but it is very shallow. That's right! Now straight on till we come to a lane."

At last they came to a winding lane. On one side there was a farm, and Roger thought it really looked exactly like his toy farm at home, even to the funny stiff trees that seemed to grow from the round piece of wood at the bottom and not from the ground itself. White celluloid ducks swam on a pond, and they quacked as loudly as real ducks, but sounded rather hollow.

As they drew nearer to Toy-Town itself Roger was surprised to see a large crowd on the road. He hooted a great many times and the people got out of the way. They were strange-looking folk – all of them toys of various sizes. Some were small and some were as large as Roger himself. There were ducks dressed up, rabbits in coats and trousers, dolls of all kinds, a clown or two, a large pink cat whose ears wagged to and fro as he walked, and many other toys.

"Oh, dear! It's market-day in Toy-Town today," said the doll, suddenly. "I wondered why there were so many people. What a nuisance! I don't expect the Hospital will be open. It shuts on Sundays and market-days."

"But Hospitals never shut!" said Roger, in surprise.

"Toy Hospitals do," said the doll. "Now I shall have to wait till tomorrow to get my leg mended. What a nuisance!"

They drove into Toy-Town. It was a marvellous place! Roger could quite well see that every house, every shop, every farm was built of bricks or meccano. But they were all a good size, far bigger than toys. There was a wooden policeman in the market-square, and he stopped Roger as he pedalled along in his motor-car.

"You're going too fast!" he said, sternly. "It's market-day today, so there's a low speed-limit."

"Oh, policeman, is the Hospital shut?" asked the doll, leaning out.

"Of course," said the policeman.

"Is there anywhere I can stay for the night?" asked the doll. "I want to get my leg mended tomorrow."

"You might try at the big farm over there," said the policeman, pointing to a fine toy-farm not far off. "I know Mrs. Straws has a few beds for visitors."

103

"Would you drive me there, Roger, and go and ask the farmer's wife if she can let me stay the night?" asked the doll. Roger at once drove over to the farmhouse and got out at the little wooden gate. Toy cows and horses were everywhere, some made of wood, some made of lead. They ran up to him like dogs and seemed delighted to see him. He pushed them away and went up to the front door of the farmhouse He knocked loudly.

Mrs. Straws came to the door. She was just like the farmer's wife in Roger's farm at home. In fact, she was *so* like her that he really wondered for a moment if she had run away and come to Toy-Town.

"What is it you want?" she asked.

"Could you let a doll with a broken leg stay here for the night?" asked Roger. Mrs. Straws shook her head.

"I'm sorry," she said, "but all my beds are quite full up tonight. It's market-day, you know, and Toy-Town is always crowded then. I'm afraid you won't find a bed anywhere at all."

Roger went back to the car and told the doll. Her big blue eyes filled with tears. "What am I to do?" she said. "I must sleep somewhere for the night."

The farmer's wife came up to the car when she saw the doll crying. "Don't upset yourself," she said. "You can easily get a box of bricks from the store-keeper in the middle of the town, and surely this boy can build you a nice little house for the night!"

That *did* sound a splendid idea! Roger climbed into his car again and drove the doll to the store-keeper's. He lived in a great barn-like building in the centre of the town. His house was stored with boxes of all shapes and sizes. When he heard what Roger wanted he took him inside at once. Roger stared at the great boxes everywhere. He saw that some contained railway-lines, some bricks, some farms ready to be put together.

The store-keeper pulled out a box and pushed it to Roger. "This will build a nice little house for one night," he said. "Don't lose any parts because I may want it back."

Roger managed to carry the box on his back. It was very big and heavy. He balanced it on his car, and then found that he couldn't possibly get in himself.

"Tell me where to go and I'll push the car along," he said to the doll. So she told him, and Roger guided the car from outside and at last came to a small field.

"This will do nicely," said the doll. So Roger put the box down on the ground and opened it. It had inside a great many small wooden bricks with little pegs to hold them together. Roger had had a building-set like that before, so he soon set to work. It was fun building a toy house that was nearly as big as a real shed!

Before he had done very much the doll said she was hungry. She gave Roger some cardboard money, and he set off to the little shops. He bought some queer-looking cakes and pies, which really felt like painted wood, but which tasted most delicious when he and the doll tried them.

Then he went on with his building and before tea-time had finished the toy house. It was very good indeed, and the doll was delighted with it.

"Now you can go and ask at that big dolls' house over there if they can spare us two beds, a table, and chairs for the night," she said to Roger. "You *will* stay with me till my leg is mended, won't you? Then you can take me back in your car tomorrow."

Roger promised that he would. He hoped his mother wouldn't worry about him, but he didn't feel he could leave the doll with the broken leg. He went off to the big dolls' house and found that the doll who lived there was a cousin of the broken-legged doll – so she was very pleased to lend the furniture they wanted. She sent her two men-servants over with it, and soon the little house that Roger had built began to look very real and cosy.

The two of them had tea together. Then Roger went out to have a look round at Toy-Town. This really was an adventure, and he wanted to see everything! The market was crowded with people and toys of all kinds.

Clockwork mice ran busily about, and little tin men on bicycles rode up and down the streets, sometimes stopping and asking the passers-by to wind them up again. Roger wound up a duck on wheels and a clockwork clown who went along head-over-heels all the time.

The animals in the market were all like toy farm animals, and they made as much noise as real ones. After he had looked at them all Roger made his way to the railway station. This was a most exciting place! Clockwork trains rushed in and out, and toy signals went up and down all by themselves. Toys got in and out of the carriages, gave up their tickets, and behaved just like people. Roger wished he could have a ride in one of the trains, but he didn't like to in case it took him too far away.

He went back at last to the little house he had built. The doll was in bed and asleep. Roger got into bed too, wondering if his mother was missing him, and very soon he was fast asleep. He didn't wake up until he heard the doll hopping about on one leg, getting breakfast.

"Hurry up!" she cried. "I'm getting so excited to think I'll have my leg mended soon. Eat your breakfast and we'll go."

Soon they were in the little car once more, and Roger drove to the hospital. He helped the doll inside, and the nurse, who was another doll, dressed in an apron and cap like a nurse, told him to wait. He sat down and watched the one-legged doll go hopping out of the room, carrying her broken leg carefully in her arms.

A great many toys came to be mended whilst he was there. A doctor stood at one end of the room and looked at all the patients one by one. There was a teddy-bear whose boot-button eyes had come loose. They were soon sewn on tightly. There was a poor little duck that had lost its clockwork key. The doctor fitted it with another and it ran off happily. There was a red dog without a tail and a blue rabbit with only one ear. The doctor sewed a new tail and a new ear on, and off they went, as happy as could be. Roger thought he could watch all day.

And then a monkey came running in – and how Roger stared! For it was his own toy monkey from home. The long-tailed creature pointed to a hole in his back, from which the sawdust was beginning to come out. Roger went red. He remembered quite well that he had caught Monkey on a nail by accident and had torn it. He had meant to ask his mother to mend him and had forgotten.

The doctor sewed up the hole quickly. The monkey was very grateful. Roger screwed himself up in his corner, to hide. He didn't want the monkey to see him there. He might tell the doctor that there was the boy who had caught him on a nail! The monkey skipped gaily out without seeing him.

Then the doctor came over to Roger, with a big needle and cotton. "What's the matter with *you*?" he asked, kindly. "Where do you want to be mended? Shall I sew you up somewhere? Or have you lost your key?"

"No, I'm quite well, thank you," said Roger, hurriedly, half-afraid the doctor might really sew him up somewhere. "I'm just waiting for a friend of mine."

At that moment in came the doll. She danced in on two legs, singing a little song of happiness.

"See!" she cried, dancing a tiptoe dance. "My leg is mended, Roger! Isn't it lovely! Oh, I do hope Mary never drops me again. I might not find a kind little boy like you again, to take me to Toy-Town. Come along. We'll go home now!"

They climbed into the car again and off went Roger, hooting through the busy streets of Toy-Town. They soon left them behind and came to the wood where Roger had found the little doll.

"You can leave me here, Roger," said the doll. "I can find my way home easily now. Thank you so much for all your kindness. I hope I see you again one day."

She threw her arms round his neck, gave him a good hug, then jumped out of the car and ran into the wood, waving her hand merrily. Roger drove on and at last came to the lane that led to his home. He drove up to the door and got out.

"Hallo, Roger!" said his mother, coming to the door. "You haven't been long! It's just about dinner-time."

"Haven't been long!" said Roger, in surprise. "But, Mummy, I've been away a day and a night. I've been to Toy-Town."

"You've been gone just an hour," said his mother, kissing him. "Go and wash your hands. You must have been dreaming!"

Well, wasn't that queer? Roger really couldn't understand it at all. *Had* he been dreaming? Or was Time quite different in Toy-Town? He couldn't make up his mind what to think.

But one day he went to see his cousin Mary, who lived at a farm about two miles away – and there he saw the doll again! He was quite sure it was the same doll he had taken to Toy-Town, though now she was smaller.

"Mary, did your doll ever break her leg?" he asked his cousin. Mary nodded her head in surprise.

"Yes, I dropped her once," she said. "How did you know? But, Roger, it was so queer, her leg got mended all by itself somehow. One day it was broken – and the next it was all right again. I can't think how!"

"Well, *I* can tell you!" said Roger, proudly. And he told Mary all about his adventures in

Toy-Town with the doll. She *was* surprised. She picked up the doll and looked at her.

And Roger saw the doll smile at him, though Mary didn't. So he *knows* his adventure really did happen, after all!

Poor Old Scarecrow!

There was once an old scarecrow who stood in the middle of a farmer's field. The farmer had made the scarecrow, and really, he looked very life-like. He had a turnip for a head, with eyes and mouth scooped out, and a piece of stick for a nose. He had an old bowler hat on his turnip head. Round his neck was a red scarf full of holes.

He wore a dirty old coat of the farmer's, and a pair of trousers so ragged that, really, it was a marvel they hung together. But they did. He had two sticks for legs and two sticks for arms, and that was all there was of him.

He stood in the field on the sloping hillside, and looked in front of him all day long. The birds were not a bit afraid of him except when the wind blew his coat and scarf about. Then they thought he was alive and flew off, frightened.

"Silly creatures!" thought the scarecrow,

scornfully. "Frightened by a bit of flapping in the breeze. Oh, dear me, what a life this is! Nothing ever happens. All I see are the foolish birds and a lolloping rabbit or two. I want some one to talk to. There are many things I think about as I stand here all day long. Surely I am not too ugly for other creatures to speak to me. What about the pixies in the hedge? Why don't they pass the time of day with me sometimes? Are they too high and mighty?"

The pixies were not too high and mighty, nor were the goblins who lived in the caves along the hillside. But they were afraid to visit the scarecrow. You see, he really was so ugly, so dirty, so ragged! So they kept away from him, and even when he beckoned to them with his stick-like hand they pretended not to see him.

Now one night something very exciting happened to the scarecrow. It was like this. He stood out there in the middle of the field, yawning and bored. It was cold and he was lonely. Only a rabbit had come near him that day, and he really was longing to talk to some one.

So when he saw two strange figures walking over his field, he was very much excited.

"They are coming to visit me!" he thought. "At last I shall have some one to talk to! How marvellous!"

But when the two people came nearer in the pale moonlight the scarecrow saw that they were almost as ugly as he was! They were witches, long and lean, bony and bent.

"Let us talk here," said one witch to the other. "No one will hear us, in the middle of this lonely field. We will sit down beside the scarecrow and whisper our secret plans."

"What a scarecrow it is, too!" said the second witch, scornfully, looking the poor scarecrow up and down. "Turnip head and turnip brains! Silly, gaping thing!"

The scarecrow was so hurt and surprised at these unkind words that he couldn't think of anything at all to say. He just stood and gaped all the more, and he felt as if his scarf was choking him.

The witches took no more notice of him. They sat down on the cold earth and began to whisper.

Now the scarecrow's ears were not much to look at, but they were very sharp, so he could hear every word that was said. And very strange was the thing that the witches talked about on that moonlit night.

"The Princess comes this way tomorrow night," whispered the first witch. "She will only be attended by two fairies, and she will be in her rabbit-carriage."

"Then we will lie in wait for her under the blackberry hedge over there," whispered the

113

other witch. "We will take her prisoner and throw the fairies with her into the nearest holly bush."

Both the witches laughed at this. The scarecrow was so amazed at what he heard that his hat fell off. Both the witches jumped up in alarm, and when they saw it was only the scarecrow's hat that had made them jump, they stared at the scarecrow angrily. The first witch picked up his hat and jammed it down so hard on his turnip head that it went over one of his eyes so that he could hardly see. But he didn't say a word. No, he knew better than that!

"No one knows of our plan," said the first witch. "Meet me here tomorrow night, friend, before the moon rises, and we will go to the hedge to lie in wait for the Princess."

They went silently down the hill together, their pointed hats showing up in the moonlight, two strange and ugly figures. The scarecrow blinked his turnip eyes and thought hard about what he had heard.

He wondered who the Princess was who was coming that way the next night. So when he saw a small rabbit venturing into the field to eat a few shoots, he called to him in his funny, woodeny voice:

"Rabbit! There is something important I must say to you. Come nearer."

The rabbit looked at the scarecrow in alarm. He lolloped just a little nearer and cocked his long ears up at the scarecrow.

"Don't flap your coat at me," he said, "or I shall run away."

"Don't be silly," said the scarecrow impatiently. "*I* don't flap it. It's only the wind. Listen, rabbit. Who is the Princess who is coming this way tomorrow night?"

"It's the Princess Peronel of Pixieland," said the rabbit in surprise. "How ever did you hear that news, scarecrow? Why, we thought only the rabbits knew, because two bunnies that pull the carriage told us. Don't you tell any one, now!"

"There's no need to," said the scarecrow. "Lots of people seem to know! There were two witches here just now, and they said that . . ."

But the rabbit didn't wait to hear any more. At the mention of the word "witches" he was off like a shot! Witches! Tails and whiskers, to think that he was out on a night that witches chose! Ooh!

The scarecrow looked at the running rabbit angrily. *Now*, what was he to do? Just as he was telling the rabbit, so that he might be able to lollop off and warn the Princess, the silly little creature must needs run away as if a hundred dogs were after him!

"Hi!" called the scarecrow, in despair. "Hi! Come back! I've got something very important to say."

But the rabbit had disappeared into a hole

and had warned all the other rabbits that witches were about. So not a single rabbit showed itself again that night, and the scarecrow shouted himself hoarse.

He began to get alarmed. Just suppose he couldn't get help in time? Just suppose the dear little Princess Peronel should really be taken prisoner by those two horrid witches! Just suppose – but the scarecrow really couldn't suppose any more.

When the sun rose, the birds came flying into the field. "Perhaps if I call and beckon to them they will listen to what I have to say," thought the scarecrow.

So he began to call to the birds in his hoarse, woodeny voice, and he flapped his arm-sleeves about to beckon them and waggled his trouser legs.

But, dear me, the birds came no nearer – no, they were frightened, and flew away at once, screeching: "The scarecrow is alive today! Beware! Don't go near him! He'll be walking down the field next!"

The scarecrow listened to their calls, and then a sudden thought came to him. He never *had* tried to walk, but just supposing he could? If he managed to walk down to the rabbit-holes he could give the warning easily then. He could shout it down the burrows.

Now, you know, scarecrows are so stiff that they cannot usually put one leg in front of

116

another. But our scarecrow began to try. He had all the day in front of him, so he had plenty of time.

First he tried to pull a leg out of the ground. How he tried! How he tugged, how he pulled!

It was no good at all. He couldn't seem to move his leg an inch. The farmer had driven the stick-legs firmly into the ground, and it was more than the poor scarecrow could do to move them. He was really in despair.

He stood gazing in front of him, feeling hot and out of breath, when he saw a peculiar thing. Not far from him he saw a little mound of earth rising. Then another. Then another. Whatever could that be?

He soon knew. A little velvet mole came peeping out of the ground, but when he spied the scarecrow nearby he gave a squeal of fright and made as if he would dive back into the earth again.

"Mole, mole, don't go," begged the scarecrow. "I won't hurt you. I really won't. Listen, two witches are planning to take the Princess Peronel prisoner tonight. Will you go and warn the rabbits?"

"What is a witch?" asked the mole. "And what is a Princess? Are they things to eat? I should like to hear of some nice new beetles to hunt for."

"No, they're not things to eat," said the scarecrow, in despair. "Oh, you silly little mole, never mind what they are. Just go and give my message to the rabbits. It's important."

"Nothing's important but food," said the mole. "I'm sorry, scarecrow, but I can't go out of my way to tell a silly message I don't understand. You'd better be careful, because I may have to tunnel right under you, and if I loosen the earth around your legs, you may tumble over. Ho ho!"

The scarecrow listened – and a bright idea flashed into his turnip head. Of course! That was just what he wanted! If only he could get his wooden legs loosened from the earth, he would be free to walk!

"Mole, tunnel right under me!" he begged. "Do. Do!"

"You'll fall on your nose!" chuckled the velvet mole. "You will! How I shall laugh!"

"Yes, you do it and laugh!" begged the scarecrow. "It is sure to be funny. Go on, mole."

So the mole dived back again into the earth and began to tunnel at top speed towards the scarecrow, throwing up mounds of earth as he went. Very soon the scarecrow felt the mole at work round his wooden legs and he knew that the earth was becoming very loose there.

The sunk sank down. Darkness came over the field. The birds went to roost in the trees and in the ivy. Still the mole worked around the scarecrow's legs, trying to make him fall down on his nose. And at last down he went, flop!

His hat rolled off and a large piece of earth went into his right eye.

But did the scarecrow mind? Not a bit! He was as glad as could be.

"Ho ho ho!" laughed the mole, and went on his way to tell all his friends what a joke he had played on the scarecrow.

The scarecrow tried to pick himself up, but it was very difficult. He tried and he tried. The night grew darker and the scarecrow felt frightened. Suppose he couldn't get down to the rabbit-holes before the moon rose? It would be too late to warn every one then, for the Princess would be taken prisoner before the moon came!

At last he managed to pick himself up! How queer he felt with his legs out of the ground! He picked up his hat and put it on.

And then he got a shock – for he saw creeping along by the hedge at the bottom of the field, the two witches! Yes, there was no mistaking their tall pointed hats.

"Too late, too late!" groaned the scarecrow in dismay. "Oh, dear, oh, dear! The rabbit-carriage will be by at any minute now!"

He tried to stagger along down the field and, dear me, once he got going, he couldn't stop! The field was steep and the slope took his legs along very fast indeed.

Suddenly he heard a scream, and he knew

what had happened. The rabbit-carriage had come along with the Princess and her attendants, and the two witches had stopped it. Down the field staggered the poor old scarecrow, and as he went, he yelled at the top of his voice:

"Beware, you bad witches! Here comes the great wizard Boolamoolahippitty-twink with his scratching nails, his pointed teeth, and his terrible spells! Ooooooooooooh! Beware! I come, I come, the terrible wizard Boolamoolahippitty-twink!"

What made him call out all this he really didn't know, but he felt that he must try to frighten the two witches somehow.

And he certainly did!

When they heard this strange song coming out of the darkness, and saw, with their green witch's eyes, the queer, stumbling figure of the scarecrow, with his bowler hat on all crooked, and his scarf flying out behind him, they felt quite sure it *was* a wizard. They had never heard of the wizard called Boolamoolahippitty-twink, and no wonder, for there was no such person – but they quite thought it must be some fearfully powerful magician, and they were frightened almost out of their lives.

They screamed loudly, jumped on the two broomsticks they had nearby, and sailed away into the sky at top speed. How glad the scarecrow was! He looked about for the Princess Peronel. There she was lying on the grass. looking as scared as could be.

"Princess," said the scarecrow, in his hoarse, woodeny voice, "Princess, I've come to . . ."

"Oooooh!" shrieked the poor Princess, in fright. "Go away, you horrid wizard! I'd rather have the two witches than you! Go away!"

"But I'm not *really* a wizard," said the scarecrow, humbly. "I'm only a scarecrow, and I must beg your pardon, Princess, for daring to come near you, ugly old creature that I am. But you see, I *had* to rescue you from those horrid witches. I couldn't get any one else to help."

The Princess sat up and looked closely at the scarecrow. She saw his funny round turnip face, his stick of a nose, his wooden legs and arms, and his ragged old clothes – and she knew he wasn't a wizard, but only a poor old scarecrow. Very soon he had told her everything, and she listened in silence.

"You must forgive me for frightening you like this," said the scarecrow. "I know I am not fit to come near such a beautiful creature as yourself, Princess – but, you see, there was nothing else I could do, was there?"

The Princess went up to the scarecrow. She put her warm little hand through his wooden arm and squeezed it hard.

121

"You must forgive me for frightening you like this."

"I think you're a darling!" she said. "You are a dear, brave, clever old scarecrow, and I want you to come to Pixieland with me and by *my* scarecrow! I grow fine peas there all the year round and the birds do steal them so. But if you are there, the peas will be safe. Will you come?"

Would he come! The scarecrow couldn't believe his ears! He couldn't believe his eyes! To think that this should have happened to him, an ugly old scarecrow! Well, well, wonders never cease.

He found his voice at last.

"I'd love to come, Princess," he said. "But I can't. No, I can't, it's no use."

"But why not?" asked the Princess in surprise.

"Because I'm too dirty," said the scarecrow, mournfully. "Much too dirty, and too ragged. I'd be ashamed to come to Pixieland like this."

"Oh, is that all that is worrying you?" asked the Princess, with a laugh. "How silly of you!"

She touched him lightly with her wand – and a strange thing happened. The scarecrow's bowler hat turned to gold. His scarf became red silk. His coat was made of thick brown satin with a thread of gold running through it, and his trousers turned to bright silver. My, he looked a real prince!

His turnip face was bright with joy as he saw all these wonderful things. The Princess touched him again.

123

"This is to make you able to walk and run like ordinary people," she said. At once the scarecrow found himself able to walk to and fro without staggering and stumbling. He was full of delight.

"Oh, Princess!" he said, kneeling down before her, his wooden legs bending quite easily beneath him, "you are too kind. Yes, I will come to be the scarecrow in your pea-patch. I shall be proud and honoured to scare away the birds for you. I shall walk all over your pea-patch and shout and wave my arms. Not a single pea of yours shall be eaten!"

"Well, that's settled, then," said the Princess, pleased. "Now, scarecrow, you shall come straight to Pixieland with me now. Look, there are my two fairy attendants with my rabbit-carriage. Go and bring them here, and you shall drive me home."

Very proudly, full of joy, the scarecrow drove the Princess and her two attendants home to the palace. Every one thought that he must be at least a Prince, so magnificent did he look in his grand clothes. It was only when they saw his turnip head and wooden legs and arms that they saw he was really a scarecrow.

Now he lives in the garden of the Princess Peronel, King of the pea-patch. The birds are frightened of him and never eat a single pea, which pleases Peronel very much. You should see the scarecrow walking up and down, waving his arms and shouting at the birds! He is so proud and so happy – but he did deserve his good luck, didn't he?

ENID BLYTON is Dragon's bestselling author. Her books have sold millions of copies throughout the world and have delighted children of many nations. Here is a list of her books available in Dragon Books:

FIRST TERM AT MALORY TOWERS	50p ☐
SECOND TERM AT MALORY TOWERS	50p ☐
THIRD YEAR AT MALORY TOWERS	50p ☐
UPPER FOURTH AT MALORY TOWERS	50p ☐
IN THE FIFTH AT MALORY TOWERS	50p ☐
LAST TERM AT MALORY TOWERS	50p ☐
MALORY TOWERS GIFT SET	£2·55 ☐
6 Books by Enid Blyton	

THE TWINS AT ST CLARE'S	50p ☐
SUMMER TERM AT ST CLARE'S	50p ☐
SECOND FORM AT ST CLARE'S	50p ☐
CLAUDINE AT ST CLARE'S	50p ☐
FIFTH FORMERS AT ST CLARE'S	50p ☐
THE O'SULLIVAN TWINS	50p ☐
ST CLARE'S GIFT SET	£2·55 ☐
5 Books by Enid Blyton	

MYSTERY OF THE BANSHEE TOWERS	50p ☐
MYSTERY OF THE BURNT COTTAGE	50p ☐
MYSTERY OF THE DISAPPEARING CAT	50p ☐
MYSTERY OF THE HIDDEN HOUSE	50p ☐
MYSTERY OF HOLLY LANE	50p ☐
MYSTERY OF THE INVISIBLE THIEF	50p ☐
MYSTERY OF THE MISSING MAN	50p ☐
MYSTERY OF THE MISSING NECKLACE	50p ☐
MYSTERY OF THE PANTOMIME CAT	50p ☐
MYSTERY OF THE SECRET ROOM	50p ☐
MYSTERY OF THE SPITEFUL LETTERS	50p ☐
MYSTERY OF THE STRANGE BUNDLE	50p ☐
MYSTERY OF THE STRANGE MESSAGES	50p ☐
MYSTERY OF TALLY-HO COTTAGE	50p ☐
MYSTERY OF THE VANISHED PRINCE	50p ☐

CHILDREN'S LIFE OF CHRIST	30p ☐
THE BOY WHO TURNED INTO AN ENGINE	40p ☐
THE BOOK OF NAUGHTY CHILDREN	35p ☐
A SECOND BOOK OF NAUGHTY CHILDREN	35p ☐

TEN-MINUTE TALES	50p ☐
TWENTY-MINUTE TALES	50p ☐
MORE TWENTY-MINUTE TALES	30p ☐
THE LAND OF FAR-BEYOND	35p ☐
BILLY-BOB TALES	35p ☐
TALES OF BETSY MAY	35p ☐
NAUGHTY AMELIA JANE	35p ☐
AMELIA JANE AGAIN	50p ☐
BIMBO AND TOPSY	50p ☐
EIGHT O'CLOCK TALES	35p ☐
THE YELLOW STORY BOOK	50p ☐
THE RED STORY BOOK	35p ☐
THE BLUE STORY BOOK	50p ☐
THE GREEN STORY BOOK	35p ☐
TRICKY THE GOBLIN	35p ☐
THE ADVENTURE OF BINKLE AND FLIP	50p ☐
THE ADVENTURES OF MR PINK-WHISTLE	35p ☐
MR PINK-WHISTLE INTERFERES	35p ☐
MR PINK-WHISTLE'S PARTY	50p ☐
MERRY MR MEDDLE	35p ☐
MR MEDDLE'S MUDDLES	35p ☐
MR MEDDLE'S MISCHIEF	40p ☐
DON'T BE SILLY MR TWIDDLE	50p ☐
ADVENTURES OF THE WISHING CHAIR	50p ☐

All these books are available at your local bookshop or newsagent, or can be ordered direct from the publisher. Just tick the titles you want and fill in the form below.

Name ....

Address ....

....

Write to Dragon Cash Sales, PO Box 11, Falmouth, Cornwall TR10 9EN.
Please enclose remittance to the value of the cover price plus:
UK: 22p for the first book plus 10p per copy for each additional book ordered to a maximum charge of 82p.
BFPO and EIRE: 22p for the first book plus 10p per copy for the next 6 books, thereafter 3p per book.
OVERSEAS: 30p for the first book and 10p for each additional book.
Granada Publishing reserve the right to show new retail prices on covers, which may differ from those previously advertised in the text or elsewhere.